YU

Victor Headley lives
Yush! is his third

Also by Victor Headley in Pan Books

**YARDIE
EXCESS**

VICTOR HEADLEY

YUSH!

PAN BOOKS

First published 1994 by The X Press

This edition published 1995 by Pan Books
an imprint of Macmillan General Books
25 Eccleston Place, London SW1W 9NF

Associated companies throughout the world

ISBN 0 330 33733 5

1 3 5 7 9 8 6 4 2

A CIP catalogue record for this book is available from
the British Library

Printed and bound in Great Britain

WITHOUT ANY APOLOGIES...

* All praises to the Almighty One for the health, strength and inspiration.

* Heartical salute to my brethren RAS HAMLE NEGASH and family; none of this could have been possible without you.

* Respeck to the X PRESS crew; Big up your attitude!

* All props to the SKANK magazine squad; keep wrecking them!

* Thank you to my family for standing by me; you all keep me balanced.

* Universal salute to all the youths in JAMAICA, CANADA, USA and ENGLAND who stand up for their rights and stay true to themselves.

* Special mention to all entertainers, past and present, whose vibrations keep us marching on.

* All respeck to REGGAE, the greatest music in the world.

* Love and respeck to all my bonafide people I couldn't mention here; you know who you are...

* Peace to all those who inspired, helped and supported me in this work. To those who missed the point and tried to diss me: check yo'self... and peace, still.

* Honour to President Mandela.

YUSH!

This is a story written in black and white. Do not attempt to adjust for colour.

MAGNUM & HERB

It's about 96 degrees inside, with the rhythm pushing it yet higher. Outside, the freezing wind makes you feel like you're in Alaska rather than the Bronx. The little shop at the corner of Tiemann Avenue and Boston Road sells the best juices and veg patties in the neighbourhood; after being up all night, nothing could be better. I take my friend Wicksy's order and step out into the arctic conditions.

The lady at the counter doesn't look up when I enter, but buries her head in a book until I'm actually standing in front of her.

"Mornin' Ma!" I say, pulling the hood off my head.

"Wait; whapp'n, man?! Long time..." she exclaimed.

After taking my order, she moved to the long, glass door units. I was only mildly surprised when my eyes fall on the cover of the book left overturned on the counter. I had heard that an East Coast publisher had picked up my first novel last year, but this was the first time I had actually seen it.

The lady returned with the two magnums. I handed her a $50 bill.

"The patties soon ready..."

"A good book dis?" I asked.

"Yeah man; 'nuff action!" she assured me.

I looked at the cover.

"Gangsta business..."

She nodded. One of the things she knows about me is that I have a base in England.

"Ah so much t'ings gwan in London?" she asked.

On the scale of things, New York probably ranks ten times

higher, but the poorer parts of my big city suffer from the very same pressure. Two years on since my first book was published in London and I realise now that its success owes a lot to the fact that it more or less captured that feeling of desperation in the inner cities, whether in England or America.

Before leaving London for Jamaica a few weeks ago, I delivered the manuscript of my third novel to the X Press. I guess I should feel more relaxed about the whole thing now, but it still feels like a new experience. After the 'heat' generated by the first book, I tried to rationalise it all and deal with the response but I certainly didn't think of pushing the point any further. A mix of popular demand and commercial/publishing pressures drove me to write two sequels.

So, here it is; the last part of the trilogy. I think I have learned a great deal about myself and other people because of these books and the reactions they caused. At first, I got really phased by the way the media jumped up and labelled me without a hearing. I guess the system has us trapped in some kind of stereotype mentality, but then when some black people attacked me for 'glorifying drugs and violence', it got me thinking...

On the other end, the youths on the streets really made me feel good, like I was doing something positive by writing my stories. As that is what they are; stories that express the black experience in the West in the 90s. And they do not glorify anything, I call them 'intelligent gangsta stories'.

I don't pay much attention to what the media says, but to all the black people who got me wrong, I'd say this: our children grow up experiencing violence everyday, whether verbal, visual or physical. This is a generation that knows more about RAMBO than PETER PAN. So, my angle is that we need to deal with the real causes of the problems we face, and realise sooner than later that only we, as black people, can solve the problems of the black community. I am no wiser than anyone else but I know that unless we can convince our children that there is something worth educating themselves for, something worth working towards, a lot of them will follow what seems like the quickest exit out of poverty and frustration.

For me, the greatest thing is to have helped to start the new wave of black writing and although I never set out to be a writer, and might not continue on this road for all I know, it feels great to be part of it.

What will I do next? Well, I think that maybe I'll try and write a different kind of story, one without guns or drugs in it, something warm and nice. See how you'll all like me then! It probably won't sell...

Before I leave the shop, the lady asks if I have heard about last night's shooting. The body count had gone up by two, she informed me. I picked up my food, said goodbye and headed out. Before the door had closed behind me, the lady was back, buried in her book.

In the car, the magnum tastes sweet and perfumed. Wicksy almost burns his tongue trying to eat his hot pattie too fast.

"Mek we get some sense," he said.

Next to food, it was definitely the best thing for resisting the cold climate. Wicksy slipped the car into gear and we started up Boston Road.

Victor Headley
N.Y.C, Spring '94

The tallest of the two white men dressed in a suit and tie sighed and looked up at the International Arrivals board once more. It had flashed the incoming flight from Montego Bay as being 'in customs hall' for the last half hour but there was still no sign of their guest.

"What's keeping him? Maybe we'd better check," he said.

His companion frowned, glanced around, thought about it.

"Maybe you're right sergeant, let's do that."

He led the way, towards the counter with the phone to Immigration. Fifteen minutes later, both officers emerged from their rescue operation. In tow was a visibly upset Detective Inspector Irwin Bell of the Jamaican Police Force, angry at his treatment by immigration officials.

"Man, can you believe it!" he exclaimed, fixing his broad silk tie.

"Very sorry sir, we had no idea..."

The tall man shrugged. The other, the more embarrassed of the two, turned to their guest, shaking his head despondently.

"You know how it is, nowadays..."

The three men walked down to the parking bay in silence.

On the same afternoon of that June weekend, two little boys conspired to 'rescue' the appetising wedding cake on the dressed-up table in front of them. They had already had a slice, like most of the guests now dancing and moving around in the

1

big hall, but as they say: 'craven'... The bigger boy leaned casually against the door. Though only six, he had mastered many of the ways of his elders; he kissed his teeth.

"This is easy, just follow me, come on."

The boy tugged urgently at his younger accomplice's sleeve. He, in a neat suit and bow tie, hesitated, aware that if anything went wrong, his mother would kill him, or as good as. He followed his senior nevertheless, crawling cautiously under the table.

"You see the pieces on the table? I'm gonna pull this tablecloth and they'll drop. You catch them, alright?"

That was the plan in any case. But it went wrong and both cake and tray fell on the unfortunate accomplice's head. Everyone turned to see what was happening...

Still dazed, the little boy heard his name called.

"Marcus!"

The ringleader had already fled, unnoticed in the confusion following the crash. Charlie mused from the corner of the room where he sat as he surveyed the havoc his son had caused.

"Let's hope the new baby's less crazy," he said in a mid-Atlantic accent.

D. smiled and nodded.

"Yeah."

Just about then, the offender arrived, his irate mother dragging him by the arm.

"Do me a favour, keep him with you. I don't know what he's going to try next."

Charlie threw his son a reproachful glance, but it wasn't genuine, and Marcus could tell the difference. He smiled mischievously and made his way to stand by his father.

"Okay Charm, just relax, I'll take care of him," Charlie said.

Charmaine walked away in her elegant dress.

2

"So, how d'you feel now?" Charlie looked at his friend. D. let out a short laugh.

"How I feel? Me jus'... on time, y'know, on time."

Charlie laughed.

"Married life can be cool, look at me."

Both men laughed heartily. Even Marcus laughed.

"Now that you're gonna get legal, you'll have to keep clean," Charlie grinned at his partner. "You know what I'm saying?"

D. knew exactly what Charlie meant. They had discussed the same point several times over the last few months, about turning the business legit. But there were still a few scores to settle. Charlie held up his hand.

"Since it's your wedding day, maybe it's not the right time."

D. shrugged.

"Wedding day? Dat don't matter, man. All I want is one t'ing an' yuh know dat."

Charlie said nothing, because he'd said it all already. D. emptied the glass in his hand. Dressed in a grey silk suit and necktie, he could have passed for a high-flying business executive. But when he spoke, his voice was a little too cold, his eyes just a little too still.

"I did wait, because yuh ask me to, t'rough the police vibes an' t'ings. But right now, time has come."

Charlie took off his hat, scratched his head. Marcus picked up the hat, his father let him have it.

"Who you gonna go after?"

D. held up his gaze.

"De yout' ah work fe we, wid me direckly. So anyone comin' after him was aimin' at me . Yuh nuh see't?"

On the streets, no one knew or was prepared to give away any names. Immediately after Sticks' shooting, D. had targeted Judge, Chin's Lieutenant. He had more than one reason to

3

avenge himself of Sticks. But was he that bold? After holding back his response to his soldier's killing for three months at Charlie's request — three months which seemed to D. like three years — he had started his move. The first approach, thanks to Linton, was not too successful. Linton set up Mona, Judge's ex, telling her to pay her former boyfriend a visit and get back in favour. That way, he reasoned, he would discover Judge's plans. Linton proved difficult to keep in check; Sticks' death had brought out the worst in him. He still listened to D. and took orders, but he was visibly on edge as if the fact that he'd been absent on the fateful night his friend was shot, still gnawed away at his heart. When Mona appeared on Linton's doorstep, bruised from a beating Judge had unleashed on her, the young soldier decided to take action. A couple of days later, D., Linton and Pablo went to pay Judge a visit. Eventually, to his disappointment, D. departed having to admit that Judge had had nothing to do with Sticks' death. The man shed no tears for Sticks, but he hadn't caused any difficulties for D. either. He would have been a fool to risk the smooth running of his business for such a hit.

D. had done a lot of thinking in those last few months. He had mourned his friend, the faithful youth who always had his back covered. When he was alive, Sticks kept things turning. Now D. missed him in many respects. Together with Charlie, D. had arranged for his lieutenant's body to be flown home for burial. The pair paid for everything and his family gave Sticks a decent funeral.

This sunny wedding afternoon in a Hampstead hotel had relaxed D. Tonight, he would act as married as he could feel. But tomorrow, the hunt would start. Someone would have to pay for Sticks' death.

"Linton suppose to call me," D. said finally.

"Yeah, where is he anyway? How come he left so early?"

"Him soon come, man," D. said cryptically.

Charlie suddenly realised that Marcus had slipped away. At about the same time a woman's voice rose a little way off in the dancing crowd.

"Ah weh dis lickle bwoy ah do?!"

Marcus was spinning on the dancefloor with his father's hat pulled down over his eyes and consequently he head-butted a large woman in the behind, rudely interrupting her calypso dance. Marcus was called to order and the dancing continued.

Charlie and D. noticed the bride coming towards them. The bridegroom was unable to resist a smile, as the attractive white-clad woman who now wore his ring approached.

"How are you feeling?" Jenny whispered in D.'s ear, a little smile on her lips. She took his arm.

'Why everybody ask how me feel?' D. wondered. He said he was okay, putting aside his earlier thoughts of revenge for the time being.

As the driver's door of the white Lexus opened, the contents of the ashtray dropped into the gutter. The driver spat out, then slammed his door shut. From where he was parked he could see the entrance to the club on the other side of the street, but his car, behind a removal van on a side street, was out of sight.

11:07pm read the clock on the dashboard. Linton glanced in the rearview mirror for a last look and patted his close-cropped hair mechanically. He leaned back. Minutes later, he spotted a silhouette pushing its way through the queue of ravers on the

5

pavement. A young woman ran across the road. As she drew parallel to the front of his car, Linton unlocked the door. She climbed inside.

"Hi!"

Her eyes looked straight at him, half-smiling. Linton smiled back.

"How yuh doin'?"

"I can't stay long..."

"Yeah man, I know."

Linton turned the ignition and steered slowly out of parking then turned right.

"Let's coast a little," he said.

The white car mingled with the Sunday night traffic. Linton manoeuvered through a couple of back streets and ended up in Homerton, speeding past the marshes.

"When did you get back?" Glenda asked, pulling on a cigarette.

Linton glanced her way.

"Friday night. T'ings took longer than I thought. Why, yuh miss me?" he added.

Glenda blew some smoke and let out a little, sharp laugh.

"The question is, did you miss me?"

"How yuh mean? I miss yuh fe real."

Past the train station, then down the lane, Linton parked alongside a row of brick houses. He still lived in Leyton, but in a different house. Linton had moved out of the place he and Sticks occupied as soon as he could after his friend's death. Puggy was nevertheless resident at the new place as he had been at the old place. D. also kept a room at the back.

Linton led the way into the house. Glenda had been there a few times already in the past two months. Linton prefered that she came by taxi to an arranged meeting point, then he would take her out after which they usually went back to his place. Glenda accepted the situation because she liked Linton and he treated her well.

Linton pushed open the communicating door and knew right away who was in. Glenda followed him into the living room. A voice coming through the stereo speakers greeted them. Back to the door, his head tilted upwards and a microphone held up in his right hand, Puggy was giving his all. The rhythm, from an old Heptones hit tune, boomed out raw and punchy. Linton observed Puggy for a moment, shrugged at Glenda and walked on through towards his room. Puggy was just finishing his verse. He turned around just in time to glimpse the pretty woman disappearing after Linton. He turned down the volume and called out.

"Yaow Linton, wha'ppen, sah?!"

"Cool, yuh know," Linton replied from his room.

Puggy was right behind. He stopped by the door, smiling broadly at Glenda as she took off her jacket. She sat on the bed under his gravilicious gaze.

"Good evening, miss," Puggy began. Then to Linton. "So, where yuh meet a nice brown gal like dat, star?"

Linton kicked off his shoes and slipped a cassette in the machine, then turned to admire Glenda.

"Ah my gal... she nice, nuh true?"

"Ah your gal, a'ready?!" Puggy smiled again at Glenda. "So, yuh have a sister, a cousin?"

Linton had to laugh. "Leave it, Puggy man. You keep singing, ah your t'ing dat."

Puggy had to retreat. Before he closed the door, Linton told him:

"Mek sure yuh sing good t'night, yuh ah entertain me an' my gal."

7

Once they were alone, Linton sat down on the bed, caressing Glenda's bare arm. The girl looked at him, blinked, looked down. Linton got up and went to a bookshelf near the bedside.

"So how's t'ings at work?" he asked.

"Okay."

Linton sat back on the bed, nodding to the tough ragga track. Next door, Puggy was still spinning dubs to sing on.

Once he had finished preparing the pipe, Linton pulled his lighter out of his pocket and burned, then handed it to his waiting woman. She closed her eyes as her painted lips closed around the glass and pulled deeply. The way the lines on her face stretched you could almost see the rush on her small, Chinese-like features. Linton came closer. Glenda was now more relaxed, her head tilted slightly back, both hands behind her on the duvet-covered bed.

"So, yuh hear any more 'bout dat shipment?" Linton asked.

Glenda took a few seconds, her eyes closed.

"No..."

"Nothing... notin' happen?"

Glenda opened her eyes, found Linton's own very close. She sighed, swallowed.

"Well... yes something."

Linton's insistent gaze probed deeper.

"Some guys came to the club during the week..."

"What kinda guys?"

Slowly, Linton's hand caressed Glenda's stomach, wandering lightly over her dress. Glenda breathed in. He stopped.

"What kinda guys?" he asked again.

"White guys, big guys, you know."

"So what happen?" Linton persisted, stroking her gently.

"Nothing. They just talked for a while then left."

"That's all?"

"Yes... Oh no, one of the guys was flashing money."

"Money?" Linton's hand came to a sudden rest.

"Yeah, money. Banknotes, you know?"

That sounded interesting.

"Then wha'?"

"Nothing. They just looked at it, then he took it back."

Glenda stretched out, leaning back until she was spread on top of the bed; Linton chilled, following some thought in his head. He got up, put down the pipe and walked to the door. Then he seemed to change his mind and sat back down on the bed, his back to Glenda. Her hand wandered under his shirt and vest, gently caressing his skin. This time, he looked down at her, serious.

"Tell me 'bout dis gyal who deal fe dem."

Glenda's hand was still toying with his muscles.

"What girl?" she asked, half-smiling.

Linton gripped her leg with his right hand, just above the knee. He pushed up a little, reached the hem of the short dress.

"De white gyal, man. Which part she live?"

The woman's face tightened for a moment at the question. Linton's hand wandered further up her leg. She swallowed before answering.

"Stamford Hill."

Linton smiled, observing her. Their eyes locked.

"Which day dem collec' from her?"

Glenda was finding it hard to concentrate. She uttered a faint sound, then whispered.

"Thursday..."

Linton eased himself down over her, she held on to him.

"Turn off the light," she whispered in his ear.

"Wha' yuh ah deal wid?" Linton kissed his teeth. Then he explored further. Glenda moaned...

9

When it was all over Glenda was already late in returning to the club. Puggy had left. Neither of them had noticed when the music had stopped.

There is curry, and then there is curry. This one was definitely the hot stuff, as evidenced by the three empty wine bottles. Two more bottles were still to be dealt with. For six people, that wasn't bad... At the far end of the table, Cole, who didn't like wine, was on to his third Tennants. The bhangra music in the background was just loud enough. When the atmosphere warmed up and the diners became a bit vocal, the music generally faded beneath the noise.

Paul's jokes had kept the three women in stitches, Simon adding a little spice of his own here and there. A nice evening out all in all, except that in the present circumstances Simon would have preferred a quiet business meeting. But as always, Paul loved to mix business with pleasure. Simon had known Paul a long time and his white friend had given him many useful contacts in circles that a black man couldn't really penetrate. But today, Simon had a crisis on his hands and Paul was at least partly responsible.

He had insisted that Simon should meet the three Spanish girls he'd invited over; another side of that Spanish property deal he'd convinced Simon to get into...

The manager came over, smiling.

"Is everything alright?"

One of the girls burst out laughing at something Paul was whispering in her ear. He tapped her on the back.

"Yeah, everything is great, " he laughed.

"Coffee?"

"I think I'd better have one, after all I'm driving."

They all laughed, even the manager who didn't really care

11

whether anyone left his establishment unfit to drive or not. They ordered four coffees. Paul caught Simon's eye and stretched. He got up.

"Girls, we have to make an urgent phone call. We'll be back shortly."

The girls smiled, nodded. One said something in Spanish, her friends laughed. Simon got up. Cole too, after briefly squeezing the leg of the long-haired girl next to him. Inside the gents, Simon washed his hands and dried them. From the urinals, Paul laughed.

"Only one of them speaks proper English, the other two don't know what we're talking about most of the time."

He crossed to the wash basin.

"What d'you reckon, Cole?"

He winked at Cole in the mirror.

"Whether she knows English or not don't matter to me," Cole said, washing his face. He took out a flannel and dried up.

"About this business..." Simon started.

Paul took out his comb.

"Simon, I know you're upset about that, but believe me, it's not down to me," he said earnestly.

Simon shook his head, frowning.

"I'm upset, the police are upset, my customers are upset. I mean, a dead 18-year-old kid is not exactly good publicity, is it?"

Paul finished fixing his hair style.

"I know that and I can assure you I got back to the man. I told him his stuff is not safe and we can't do business until he can guarantee."

Hands in his pockets, Simon sighed.

"Look; this man, I'd like to meet him. I told you!"

"Yeah, I know, but it's not like that. I mean, this guy is a big

12

businessman, very private. You know what I mean? You know how these blokes are. It's only because he's known my family for years that I got to him."

Cole offered a pack of cigarettes. They lit up.

"Okay, you understand that I must be able to guarantee my product as safe. That's why I hesitated before getting involved with that shit. Coke, I can check for myself. But H. man, that's a a little heavy. You know what I mean?"

He paused.

"And another thing; I can't risk flogging the rest of that shit. I stand to lose a lot of money."

"Oh, I don't know. Maybe the shit's not that bad. Maybe the kid was already sick," Paul remarked.

"Gimme a break, Paul! One dead, and two in the fuckin' hospital, in intensive care!"

"Alright, mate. What can I say?"

Paul looked genuinely sorry. He continued.

"Look Simon, these things happen. But on the other hand, if you don't sell it, somebody else will. There's just too much money in it."

Simon nodded, still feeling uneasy.

"So what about our trip, you still on for next month?" Paul asked.

"Yeah, yeah. I'll make it."

"Good, I'm going to book it this week."

He stretched.

"Let's get back to the ladies. I want to go clubbing to loosen them up a bit. You know what I mean, Cole?"

Cole smiled.

"I'm with you, man."

"Give us a minute, Paul," Simon said.

"Okay."

Paul left.

"What do we do now?" Cole asked.

Simon was staring in the mirror, thinking. He smoothed back his hair, checked the pony tail at the back. The scar on his left cheek still showed neatly, no matter what he did to try and mask it. He turned to Cole.

"That fuckin' guy, I wonder how much he's making as the middle man. That's the only reason he doesn't want me to get to the boss." As an afterthought he added: "For all I know, he recuts the stuff himself to stretch it. That way he earns from both sides!"

Simon felt bitter. Maybe he shouldn't have gotten involved with smack, as he had thought at first. Yet Paul was right; despite the risks, it was too profitable to ignore. All that cheap H. flooding the market... And Simon needed every pound he could get his hands on to finish building his gym before the autumn. Once that was over, he could relax a little.

"What about that cop business?"

Simon looked at his friend, jaw tight. He didn't need reminding of the vexing episode earlier that week. Things were getting just too heavy lately. With the junky's death, it sounded a little too much of a coincidence. Yet, the local 'pimp' — as he privately liked to call the Detective who taxed him — had come to him first and shaken him, then that other guy had come from nowhere with his bullshit badge and started acting tough.

"What the fuck is going on, Cole?"

The question defined exactly how Simon felt. Cole could feel it too. He scratched the back of his head, below the crown of short dreadlocks.

"We've got to cut that shit out. We were doing okay before. That's what I think anyway."

Cole watched for Simon's reaction.

14

"Yeah you're right... but I want to stay on for this Spanish deal, that's the big bucks. " He smiled. "...Or pesetas."

Serious again, Simon pointed at Cole.

"We've got through problems before that didn't rock the boat. I have a feeling we could get some fully legal fronts by next year."

He sounded optimistic, despite all the signs around him that something serious was happening. Cole breathed in deeply.

"I hope you're right."

"Come on, let's get back and finish the night."

They left the gents. The general mood was for a tour on the town. It took the six of them until 6.30 the next morning to agree on calling it quits.

The following day, a Friday, a phone call woke Simon in bed like a bolt of lightning; one of his 'safe houses', Julie's place, had been hit. She was unhurt. Simon cursed and went to wake up Cole who was sleeping in the next bedroom. He ordered him to send the Spanish girls home. He'd be back later. By the time he had showered, Simon had more than a hangover to deal with.

S top messing about!" Jenny was left holding the jacket as her son ran out of the living room giggling. She sighed, annoyed, marched through after him and found him perched on the bed, his dark little eyes squinting at her. As she approached, the little boy screamed and threw his arms around the sleeping man beside him. There was a shifting under the sheets and a groan. Jesse held tight to his father's neck, resisting Jenny's attempts to pull him away.

"No!" he shouted.

Dragged out of his sleep by the commotion, D. turned and raised two sleepy eyes above the sheet. His son was calling out.

"Daddy! Daddy!!"

It wasn't really Jesse's habit to make trouble in the morning, yet today he seemed determined to give his mother a hard time. She managed to pull him down but he cried out.

"I want to stay with Daddy!"

"Look, I'm late as it is. Put on your jacket."

Jenny was about to get firm with her hard-headed son. D. stretched, then propped himself up on one elbow.

"What happen, boss?" he asked Jesse.

The little boy got up off the floor and looked straight at his father.

"I want to stay with you."

D. laughed, rubbing one hand over his face.

"Just leave him man, me deal wid him."

Jenny chuckled.

"You? You're too busy for that."

But D. insisted.

16

The little boy, sensing he had won his case, sat back on the bed by his father.

"You gwan ah work, mek him stay."

"I've paid the child-minder already," Jenny said, making a last check on her hair in the mirror. An early sun was peering through the half-opened blinds.

"Don't worry 'bout dat. Him haffe spar wid me more time."

Jenny smiled, sat on the bed.

"Good, you're starting to take your responsibilities seriously." She caressed D.'s bare chest, lightly.

"Wait; I t'ink seh yuh late," he reminded her.

She got up.

"You sure you don't want the car?"

"Nah man. You gwan. Linton coming fe me."

Since passing her test the previous month, Jenny had been driving the Audi to work. D.'s new car was due the following week.

Jenny threw a last glance at her son and started out.

"I'll be late this evening. I've got to go visit Soni."

"Yeah man, tek yuh time," D. said flopping back down on the pillow.

Jenny left. D. had a fleeting thought for Soni, hospitalised for the third time in as many months. After the shooting that killed her man, she had spent the next two weeks in observation. She had been lucky to escape with only one pellet in the shoulder, but she had suffered a nervous breakdown and the doctors gave the baby little chance of surviving. But she hung on inside and out, keeping Sticks' unborn child alive against all the odds. Jenny had faithfully attended to Soni, giving her support and hope. That terrible night of blood had brought the two women closer in a tragic sort of way which helped both of them to cope with the memory. Jenny, though she did her best to help Soni, had also been deeply affected by Sticks' death. That night she had remained strong throughout the dreadful hours following the shooting; accompanying Soni to the hospital, facing the police questioning. Yet a few days later, the stress had caught up with her and she broke down, crying uncontrollably. Her sister called a doctor who recommended sedation and total rest for a couple of weeks. After that, she started back at work but the experience had changed her forever. D. could tell this by the way she kept quiet for long periods, blinking nervously at the sound of gunshots on the TV. The nights, especially the first few weeks after the shooting, had been difficult. Jenny would wake up in the dark and throw herself trembling on D., shaken by the same nightmarish memory. D. had stayed with her most nights since then, especially since Donna, D.'s other woman, had flown out to Jamaica shortly after. Sticks' death had fuelled the tension that had grown between Donna and D. over the weeks preceding it. Because she couldn't get D. to settle down the way she wanted him to, Donna had been moody and D. in turn tended to spend more time out, to avoid what he saw as pointless arguments. Still, she realised how much more tension Sticks' death would bring and they both agreed that the holiday she had been meant to take with the children was now due. D. drove Donna, Cindy and Avril to the airport in the last week in May. Leroy had been in Jamaica since the previous month and would meet them in Kingston. Apart from a well-deserved break and the joy of returning home after years away, Donna was on a mission. D. had charged her, in conjunction with Leroy — who was supervising the construction of his house out there — to find a piece of land and to organise the building work. Aside from Donna's constant reminders, D. knew he should start investing back in Jamaica. A nice house in one of the choice areas around the St Andrew Hills would be a good start.

"Go an' turn on de radio," D. told his son, who was delighted at being given permission to do what he usually got into trouble for. Jesse hopped off the bed and went to the set. He'd discovered how to operate both the tuner and the cassette decks and it seemed to be his greatest pleasure.

"Turn it down, man!" D. cried out as the music came through deafeningly loud.

Jesse turned down the volume. A classic rock steady bass bounced out. The morning revival sessions of the community stations were always a welcome way to start the day. D. lay there for a while, turning the events of the last few days in his mind, taking stock. For him also, Sticks' killing had brought home a lot of facts. The brutality of his lieutenant's end had shaken his consciousness. All the more so because both his women had gone hysterical, convinced that he would end up the same way unless he gave it all up. They had both pressured him non-stop since that night. Yet he couldn't give it up, he knew that. How could he?

The last Friday of June looked set to be sunny and warm. After a lengthy, painful winter, everyone welcomed the longer days and mellow nights.

The phone called D. back to the present.

"Yeah, wait, wha'ppen sis? "

Sweetie was on the line.

"Who is it?" Jesse hovered around the phone interested.

"Alright, yeah man. I soon come. You talk to him."

D. gave a beaming Jesse the phone and let him converse with Sweetie. Meanwhile, he got up and went to the kitchen in his shorts. Jesse came to join him shortly after.

"Yuh finish talkin' to auntie?" D. asked.

The little boy nodded and sat at the kitchen table opposite his

19

father. D. sipped some hot tea, then got up to fry some eggs and plantain. Jesse had had breakfast with his mother but ate with D. all the same. Afterwards D. sat him in the living room with a cartoon video while he had a shower and dressed. Then father and son sat to watch TV for a while. Jesse absorbed himself in the Western, now and then pointing the plastic gun on his lap at the screen to join in a shootout. D. was busy punching figures on a calculator, writing totals on a slip of paper. He called Pablo to check on some accounts. The doorbell rang shortly after; it was Linton.

"Wha' ah gwan, don?" Linton walked in, sporting a green and white corduroy outfit.

"Cool."

Linton sat down and poked Jesse in the ribs. He got himself shot by the plastic gun for that.

"So yuh ah babysit, man?"

D. smiled.

"Yeah, yuh know. My bwoy refuse to follow him madda dis mornin'."

Linton turned to Jesse.

"Yes I, yuh haffe stay wid de man dem. Touch me nuh!"

Serious, Jesse touched fists with Linton.

"Anyt'ing new?" D. asked, pulling a plastic bag out of the wall unit drawer.

Linton took the rizla offered.

"T'ings cool a way, but de beast dem ah get busy. Comin' like the sun bring dem out!"

"What about de Chiney gal?" D. rolled his spliff.

"She good, man, tell me ev'ryt'ing I want fe know," Linton said.

D. nodded as Linton volunteered the latest information from Glenda.

Thanks to her, Linton and two other soldiers had been able to carry out a raid on the girl that worked for Simon in Stamford Hill. Her house in a relatively residential part of the area had been used as a distribution point that turned over a considerable amount of money weekly. The move went down nicely, the girl had offered little resistance once she got her mouth busted by a gun butt. Linton had walked away with a few grand in his pockets.

D. wanted to concentrate on planning the downfall of his enemy now he was sure that that was where the hit had come from. Linton too. He had been there the night Sticks had cut Simon in the face. Linton had told D. about his feelings even before they approached Judge. Ironically, since that same night, Linton always intended to go back for the girl he had so conveniently used as a human shield. Shortly after New Year, he went back to the club, out of sight, and waited for her. Glenda immediately recognised him and froze at first. Linton needed all his charm and powers of persuasion to lower her defences and get her to talk. He acted real smooth, told her how much he liked her, how pretty he thought she was and eventually she agreed to a date. Linton kept up the pressure, explaining that although they had business problems with Simon, Glenda's employer, that didn't prevent them from seeing each other. Glenda took a little time to warm up to the tall, good-looking man but then Linton had a way with women. She never actually said that she knew Simon was behind Sticks' death, but Linton interpreted her silences whenever he mentioned it. He answered her only query by saying that his friend was dead and nothing would bring him back. He just had to go on living and forget about it. He didn't know for sure whether Glenda believed he harboured no thought of revenge but anyway, she soon opened up to him.

21

She talked about her singing and modelling careers which Simon had helped her to launch. She worked at the Satellite wine bar on weekends and also did some 'public relations' work when asked. Linton sweeted her up, kept her talking. In that way he learned that, despite being grateful for Simon's help and support, Glenda had never really forgiven him for abandoning her for a white girl. After that, it was strictly business.

Linton's control of Glenda proved invaluable to D. He was carefully planning his final move.

"You sure she can't turn over?" D. asked, blowing out some smoke.

Linton lit up his spliff.

"Nah man," he laughed, amused at the idea and added: "Dat gyal mad over me."

D. nodded.

"Nice. We gwan hit dem dis Sunday."

Linton looked at him without saying anything. That seemed to please him.

D. looked at his watch. He had promised Sweetie that he would pass by early.

"I want to do a few moves," he told Linton.

Outside, Linton opened the rear door of his car and let Jesse in. The little boy settled back on the big seat, taking in the music while the two men tended to their business. For lunch, they stopped by the Caribbean restaurant where they found a small crowd in an irate mood. GB, the owner, was standing by the door. He told D. and Linton that a youth that had been standing outside the restaurant had just been taken away by plain clothes police.

"De man dem jus' stop de car, two ah dem come out an' grab him, t'row him in de car an' tek off." GB explained indignantly.

"Who de yout' is?" D. asked.

"Me nuh even know him name." GB paused. "De man dem seh one black police did deh ina de car," he added.

"Eenh?!" Linton exclaimed.

"Black police? Uniform?" D. asked.

"Nah man, plain clothes. Hold on."

GB turned away and shouted out, signalling towards a small group of women outside the grocers across the road.

"Bess! Bess!"

One of them, slim with a full head of frizzy black hair, came over.

"Tell de don about de black police," GB requested.

The girl looked at D.

"Yes, ah true. One black man did deh ina de passenger seat. Me see him good, t'rough I was jus' crossing over."

"Wha' him look like?" D. asked the girl.

Bess was only too eager to fill D. in. She gave him a full description.

"He was wearing darkers, a blue suit and tie. Him have a moustache, short beard, short hair."

Linton was frowning. He smirked.

"Weh dem t'ink dis is; Beirut? Dem cyaan jus' kidnap people so."

That was exactly the opinion of the dozen or so people outside the restaurant. The incident had a bad feel to it.

D. stepped inside with his son and ordered. Linton stayed outside for a short while before joining them. They sat. Jesse munched on a fried dumpling, having extracted from his father the promise to go buy french fries at the McDonald's later.

"Dat gyal check fe me, y'know," said Linton after a taste of his saltfish and cabbage.

"Which gyal?"

23

"Bess, man. She look neat, don't?"

D. agreed that she looked 'neat'. Linton told him Bess had arrived three months earlier and that he had his eyes on her. Apparently things were getting on nicely between them.

"Yuh know seh she ah Indian sista?" Linton asked.

D. looked up from his plate and swallowed.

"Which Indian? Charlie Indian?"

"Yeah man. Yuh nuh see how she look coolie?!"

She did look like Indian. Linton said she was coming to visit him on Sunday. He grinned.

"Ah my girl dat."

GB returned from outside, still cursing about the kidnapping.

"Bwoy, me ah tell yuh; t'ings ah get dread 'round yah."

He returned to his kitchen. D. and Linton finished eating and checked out.

Completing a u-turn, Linton sounded his horn and pointed to Bess on the pavement with her friends. She waved and smiled back at him. They drove by Leroy's record shop. His helpers were in charge while he was in Jamaica, but he regularly called to check on business. The place seemed as busy as any Friday. D. purchased a couple of 45s and an LP and left a message to tell Leroy that he would phone on Sunday night.

Back in the car, D. stretched and looked up towards the sun.

"Leroy nah come back fe now, it look."

"I was t'inking of takin' a little trip ah Yard by Christmas," Linton said.

He explained that he'd been longing for a break to visit his family, soak some sun and spend some money on property maybe. D. agreed that it would be a wise move. He himself would fly out for a few weeks as soon as everything was sorted out, he said. He instructed Linton to drive him to his barber on West Green Road.

"So wha', yuh ah come to Sweetie later?"

"Wha' ah gwan?" Linton asked.

"Jus' a meetin' about de festival next month. Charlie promoting Fly an' Puggy down deh."

"Bwoy, I suppose to go an' check de Chiney gal, yuh nuh see't...? I could cancel her still," Linton added, "no big t'ing."

D. shrugged.

"Nah man, de meeting ah jus' music business. You go an' see her, pick her brain, find out if everyt'ing clear fe Sunday. De bwoy done now. "

"Bettah we dus' de whole ah dem," Linton said.

D. nodded.

The barber salon was almost empty but for an elderly man attended to by the assistant, and two youngsters, one of them in the chair. The boss greeted D.

"Wha'ppen sah? Long time."

"Yeah. Still, my hair grow slow, yuh know." D. smiled. The boss laughed.

"A'right. Mek I finish dat young man. I soon come to yuh."

"Tek yuh time," D. said as he sat on one of the chairs, Jesse by his side. "Yuh want a cut too?" he asked Linton.

There wasn't enough on Linton's head for that. The tall man smiled. They sat for a while, the music on the small square speakers in the top corners of the room dispensed vintage ska music. Jesse's head was bobbing to it. Linton's mobile rang.

"Yaow! Yes baby, wha' ah gwan?" he answered.

His haircut completed, the youngster got up to leave. He dusted himself down and took a deep long look at his 'fade' in the mirror, from all angles. Then he grinned, paid the 'artist' and stepped out with his friend.

"Ready now," the barber announced, picking up a fresh gown for his client.

"I want yuh touch my boy, lickle bit," D. said pointing at his son's head.

Jesse's hair wasn't long; it only needed shaping. The barber lifted the little boy up and placed his thin frame in the large leather chair.

"Okay, I'll be there... Nice".

Linton pushed back the phone into the top pocket of his shirt. He explained to D. that Glenda had just called to ask him to pick her up at 11pm instead of 9. That now left him enough time to go and check associates of his in south London who were interested in a deal. Jesse was staring in the big-frame mirror, his little face serious. The barber soon finished with him.

"Bes' you go and do dat move deh," D. told Linton as he got up to take his son's place in the chair. "I'll mek my way home."

"Yuh sure?" Linton asked, "I can wait you know, don."

"Cool, man. My boss here will call taxi fe me."

D. leaned back and entrusted his head to the barber.

"Alright, so wha'... Later," Linton said.

"Yeah man. After de meeting I gwan to the Spot. Meet me 'round deh."

"Seen. Respeck. Lickle Don..." Linton pointed to Jesse.

Linton stepped out of the barber saloon and into his car, driving off into the approaching dusk. The barber's work was fine and D. looked sharp when he was done with him. In fact, with similar haircuts, father and son looked even more alike. Back home, Jenny couldn't help a proud smile as both her men stepped in. Jesse ran to her.

"Mummy, Daddy take me McDonald's."

Some of the house numbers were hard to make out, but not this one; a large illuminated '58' emblazoned above the front porch. Thanks to the large, colour A-Z streetfinder, the road had been easy to locate. The man parked a little way past the house and switched off the engine. The dashboard said 10.47pm. In the mirror, the man straigthened up his tie and smoothed up his moustache with his right thumb and forefinger. He stepped out of the car and locked the doors with the alarm remote button. The night was mellow but not that quiet. Three cars passed by, looking for parking. A fourth one came up, a loud ragga bassline preceding it. It slowed down as the driver located the house he was looking for. The man started up the street slowly, watching a couple heading for the very house he was due to visit. That was a good sign; whatever was going on inside it would ease his way in. He was all in favour of a smooth approach tonight anyway. Music was coming from the front of the house. Well-dressed people were arriving. It sounded like some sort of celebration. Crossing the road, the man followed the small group of people now making their way through the gates of number 58. They were all nicely attired, the women with expensive-looking jewellery and stylish outfits. The front door opened, the man started up the few concrete stairs and through the hallway of the house. His cream suit, black shirt and purple tie struck a somewhat distinctive note against the colour match and style of the other guests. But at least he was dressed up. He smiled at the serious-looking pair of young men manning the inside door and walked in. Once inside, he quickly took stock of the layout. After picking up a drink at the bar in the lit-up lounge, he leisurely crossed the room — half-full with guests — and made his way towards the back room where the music was pumping loud. There he settled against the door, observing the comings and goings, sipping his drink. The semi-dark room was alive with swaying bodies. The rhythms were lively, mixed tight. Newcomers entered, greeting acquaintances who were already there: all the usual scenes of a happy social occasion. Silhouettes of the revelling women attracted the man's attention for a while. To the right, the bar was busy. Looking around the place, the man's keen gaze scanned faces and profiles, lingering a fraction longer on one or two. Discreetly, he watched the set up. Above the bar, a painted banner read: 'Happy Birthday'. The man smiled to himself. The flavour of the brandy titillated his palate, the warmth of strong alcohol filled the pit of his stomach. After a good half hour of observation, he felt it was time. Lightly, he stepped back across the room, excusing himself as he bounced a short, pretty woman in a white dress.

"That's alright," she said with an inviting smile.

The man smiled back, stood her gaze for a moment before turning back towards the bar behind which a couple of women were busy serving. Some of the guests were gathered around the long table to the right, where fried fish, jerk chicken, hard dough bread and salad were spread out. The man deftly picked up a paper serviette from the table. Turning away he took something from inside his jacket and wrapped it neatly in the serviette, pushed it in his right pocket then crossed the busy room, leisurely, out to the corridor.

Two men leaned casually against the walls, one on either side of the stairwell leading downstairs. As the man in the cream-coloured suit approached, they stopped chatting. The first 'guard' looked young, slim, wearing a baseball cap low on his forehead. The guest addressed the other man, a squat, balding man with an unfriendly face.

"Nice party. So, how old him is now?"

The other man stared at him, serious.

"Yuh cyan go down; private quarters."

He was polite, but cold. The guest sized him up casually before taking a sip of his brandy.

"I need to talk to de boss. Tell him a long time friend come fe him."

But the balding guard had strict orders. He shook his head.

"I give him de message. You wait here."

"Alright. Watcha now."

The guest took his right hand out of his pocket, brought out the folded serviette and handed it to the guard.

"You give him dat. Him will see me."

The guard took the 'message', frowning and looked at it. Finally, after a quizzical glance at the guest, he turned and stepped down the stairs. The younger guard eyed the guest suspiciously. He was waiting, leaning against the wall. He finishd his drink. A couple of minutes later, the balding man reappeared. He took a long look at the smiling guest, at his clothes.

"You can go down," he said finally

"Nice," the guest nodded.

He placed his empty cup on the metal bannister and left the two men to their guard duties.

Descending the spiral staircase, the man ended up in the large living room. Another man, another guard, sat on a chair in front of the TV, smoking. He looked casually up at the guest but didn't move. The music wafted down into the room from upstairs. The half-dozen people seated there were obviously celebrating. On the coffee table, bottles of various drinks, some full some empty, were lined up. Another TV, wide-screened on a thick, chrome stand, occupied most of the left hand wall. The window at the back was open. A few people stood in the garden chatting. As the man in the cream-coloured suit stepped up, the conversations slowed down. He felt all eyes on him. Confidently, he walked to the centre of the room, looking around, apparently admiring the furnishings. Finally, he stood in front of the sofa and smiled at the straight-faced man seated between two pretty girls.

"Wha'ppen sah, long time." The guest sounded genuinely happy to see the man. He however — short, dark complexion and wearing a heavy-looking gold chain — didn't seem half as pleased. Everyone else was silent.

Seemingly oblivious to the lack of response, the guest continued.

"I come a long way fe check yuh. Yuh know seh I nevah know today is your birt'day?! Still, best wishes all de same. "

The man's tone was cordial. He stretched out his hand and picked up the open wallet on the table.

"I tek dat back."

The man on the sofa watched the guest slip the wallet in his jacket pocket.

"What yuh doin' yah?" the man with the gold chain asked finally.

"Bwoy, I jus' takin' a lickle holiday." The guest turned to his right, smiled broadly at the big man in the chair. "So wha'ppen Bigga, lookin' healt'y, man."

Bigga didn't smile back. His expression betrayed his puzzlement. Two other men, well-dressed, one with a hat, sat on the other side, each with a woman beside him. The second man, shaven-headed, had a large spliff in his right hand, smoke rising up from it. The warm party atmosphere had cooled a few degrees since the unexpected guest entered the room.

"So Joseph, yuh nah offer me a drink, man?"

Joseph pointed to the table.

"Help yuhself."

The man deliberated a little before opting for a half-full bottle of overproof rum. He sipped some out of the glass, savouring the taste.

"Yeah man, ouno live good up here!" he said, admiring the place.

The comment was less than innocent. Joseph knew that.

"How yuh find me?" he asked.

The man laughed.

"I see your picture ina book an' I jus' ask fe your address."

It sounded that simple. The man looked around the room once more.

"In fact, I saw all ah ouno picture in de book," he added. His gaze settled briefly on the shaven-headed man.

"Judge, right?!" he said. "How yuh doin', man?"

Less than enthusiastic, especially because he didn't know him, Judge answered:

"Fine, fine..."

The man took a sip more.

"I went to see your boss las' mont', yuh know."

Judge who stared at him, said nothing.

"Yeah man, dem send me to America so I tek time to visit him. Him nah come outta jail fe now, it look like..."

The fact that Tony Chin wouldn't be tasting freedom for years seemed to please him somehow. As no one was saying anything, the man turned back to Joseph.

31

"An' now, dem send me yahso, as a..." He searched for the word. "...Consultant."

"So wha'? Yuh get promotion?" Joseph spoke finally.

"How yuh mean, right now I come to represent de Jamaican Force ina Englan'."

It wasn't good news. Bigga twitched uneasily in his chair. The women in the room could feel the vibe wasn't good, they didn't move. For the first time, the man seemed to notice the little white mound on the table, on Joseph's side. Slowly, he leaned over and dipped his forefinger in it. He tasted the powder and cleared his throat.

"Mmmm... good stuff man."

He sounded like a gourmet tasting a fine meal. Joseph continued staring at him. Laughing, the man said:

"It's part of the job, yah know what I mean?"

Joseph knew what he meant. The man walked around the chairs, went to the bay windows and turned around, the smile he had carried since coming in had disappeared.

"So you wonder why I come see yuh...?"

He wasn't expecting Joseph to answer.

"...Well, it's like this, t'rough ouno deh ah foreign ah run de place red, de Englishman dem send fe some help. Dat's what I am here for."

He paused to finish his rum.

"The white man dem don't like all dis shooting business whe' ah gwan. Yuh understan'?"

"So why yuh come to me?" Joseph asked. "I don't have notin' to do wid dem t'ings deh."

The man's smile reappeared.

"Joseph man, I don't want you to feel that is you alone I check. I gwan visit everybody." He added: "Is only t'rough me an' you ah ol' friend, so I came here first."

The 'friendship' he was talking about limited itself to a couple of years spent in the same class in a Kingston primary school. Joseph sighed, tried to call on that 'friendship' memory.

"Look man, come back an' check me ina de week. Me an' yuh reason."

The man stroked his short beard and explained:

"Alright, but yuh mus' understan' how dis t'ing go; dem send me on a mission, so I have to do dis job. De white man dem tired fe run after de lickle bwoy dem whe' juggle 'pon de corner. Now dem want de big fish dem. Yuh see whe' me ah come in?"

It all sounded like really bad news. Joseph looked straight at his 'old friend', still reeling from the shock of seeing him again.

"Anyway, I just wanted to let you know." The man walked back towards the table, put down his glass. "I know is your birt'day still, so I don't want to spoil it, seen?"

That, he had definitely already done.

"I gone now," he concluded, "have a nice time."

With that, the man had a last look around the room and started towards the stairs. Nobody had moved since his entrance. The spliff in Judge's hand was out, Bigga still had a half-full glass in his. Joseph didn't even say goodbye.

Upstairs, the party was in full swing. People were still arriving. By the door, the woman in the white dress he had earlier bounced observed the man as he stepped out.

"You leaving already?" she asked.

He smiled.

"That's because I didn't have no pretty girl to talk to..." he said, moving a little closer towards her. After all, he'd done what he came to do. 'After business, pleasure,' he thought.

"So, you know Joseph?" the woman asked.

"Yeah man, we used to go school together..."

Iknow dat gyal, yuh know!" Pam exclaimed, pointing at the screen. She, like everyone else in the room, was transfixed on the television.

"Which one?" Sweetie asked.

"You miss her, man! Beg yuh rewind lickle bit," Pam asked Charlie.

Obligingly Charlie rewound the video. He had already watched the programme a couple of times, but the topic had sparked a lively debate tonight and now Pam had recognised someone from back home.

"See her deh?" Pam pointed as the action replayed.

"Yeah man, wha' she name again?" Bess knew her too. She tried to recall.

"She used to live 'pon Beckford Street." Pam definitely recognised her.

"I cyan 'member her name... I soon tell yuh."

Sweetie was searching her memory for the face.

"Yuh know Richie?" Pam asked her.

"Which Richie?"

"Big Richie, man, from Edgewater."

Sweetie knew him.

"A'right, ah fe him baby madda. Yuh know her, man!"

"Ooh, yuh mean, wha' dem call her again...? Bounty? Yeah man."

"Yes, de same one."

Sweetie thought the girl had changed a lot.

Charmaine came back down from upstairs where she had tucked a relecutant Marcus in bed. The programme, an in-

34

depth look at the so-called Jamaican drug connection, was prime-time viewing and had kicked up a storm in the black community. It wasn't the first of its kind. They all seemed to be part of an overall strategy to label black people and perhaps try to justify some immigration practices. Apart from the official repercussions it brought down, the media as a whole took positions on either side, some supporting the film, others condemning it as less than objective. In their households, the pubs, the domino rooms and even the schools, the debate went on. Almost every black home had recorded the programme.

"Man, ain't nobody gonna want to visit the island after that," Charlie sighed.

In his chair, sipping his drink, D. shook his head.

"Dem man deh biased, man."

To his right, Piper shook the ash off his spliff before lighting it again. He had arrived at Charlie's late, after they had all already eaten, to answer any questions about the forthcoming festival and soon everyone involved knew what their roles were. The big open-air show Piper was organising was scheduled for the weekend of July 23rd, three weeks away.

The dread had decided to set up a Rastafari Birthday Festival, and managed almost single-handedly to co-ordinate the whole thing. The two community radio stations involved were doing a good promotion job. With the increasingly hot weather, Clapham Common was likely to be rammed on the day. Charlie and D. were involved as sponsors, and Sweetie was in charge of the stalls, allocating bookings and organising the food and drinks supplies for the artists. Puggy and Firefly were also billed to make an appearance at the Festival, among other major acts. As manager of the two artists, Charlie was involved in that side of the event as well. Meanwhile, the two artists concentrated their attentions on the programme, as did Ricky,

Firefly's friend. The two youths usually hung together, especially since the shooting incident a few months back. After they had been in hiding for almost two weeks, Charlie received Firefly's call and arranged for a lawyer to explain his innocence to the appropriate authorities. On the whole, things got straightened out rather well. The Asian shopkeeper had a close brush with death, but he recovered. Firefly and Ricky were eventually exonerated. As for Donovan, who fired the shot, no one had seen him since. As they say, a hundred miles and still running...

The whole affair had gotten Firefly closer to Charlie and to D. also — who supported and encouraged him to face the pressure. The young MC was a quick learner. He had gotten wiser and more mature in the last year or so.

"Ghetto people always get the blame!" Bess cried out. She was incensed by another tendencious allegation from the TV commentator.

"Every t'ing under the sun dem blame yard man for," D. said.

Piper drew some smoke, chuckled. Charlie sneered, disgusted by the programme's bias.

"They want to make people believe we're the first ones to bring shit over here, man."

Piper nodded.

"Dem programme will just stir up racism," he said. "The system get scared when black man get rich."

Everyone agreed that the film was doing a good job of scaring its audience. The next hour after the programme's end was spent arguing the case. Finally Sweetie stretched and said she was leaving.

"Alright dread, me check dem people an' get back to yuh by Monday," she told Piper.

"Cool me sistren. Walk good."

Pam and Bess followed Sweetie. She was driving Lee's car while he was away in New York and would drop them home. After they left, Charmaine retired. Charlie changed the cassette. Turning to his two artists, he pointed out:

"This show is important for both of you. There's gonna be a crew shooting the whole thing, so you've got to be perfect."

Puggy, self-confident as usual, assured his manager that he was going to 'blow up' at the show. They laughed. Piper quipped that, in that case, Puggy would have to perform last. Firefly said he'd be ready.

"How de new track go?" D. asked him.

"It will be ready by Monday. They're remixing it tomorrow."

As part of a strategy to put some of their earnings to good use, Charlie and D. had financed the setting up of a recording studio at the local community centre where Firefly's uncle worked. To the aspiring young musicians of the area, it had been a god-sent opportunity and the workshops held there were immensely popular. Firefly had been appointed manager of the project and he took his job seriously. That way, between school and his own muscial work he was quite busy.

When Ricky and he got up to leave, Puggy said:

"Call me tomorrow, you an' me rehearse some new lyrics I have."

Piper left soon after. Charlie said he'd contact him on the Sunday.

"Pablo don't call in yet?" Puggy enquired, sticking two rizlas together.

"He's probably gonna stay down there till tomorrow," Charlie said.

Pablo and Linton took turn to travel outside London to see to the outfit's business interests up country. The rest of the time, Pablo and Puggy worked as a team. After Sticks' untimely departure from the scene, Puggy had insisted on being brought in and, since Linton had now taken over his friend's job, Charlie agreed. Strangely, it was D. who had tried to advise the young singer to stick to his craft. He felt that since Puggy had talent he should concentrate on music and try to avoid getting too deep into the game. But Puggy had also been affected by his cousin's death. Up until then, the runnings had all been exciting and fun, glamorous even. After Sticks' death, although he remained basically the same, there was a new edge to his personality, a cold cynicism now belied his youth.

D.'s mobile phone rang, he picked up the call.

"Yeah? Hallo...? Can you hear me?"

The line cut. It was Sherry calling, but the battery was flat.

"I gwan call her back," D. said. He went to use Charlie's home phone. On his return he asked Charlie:

"Yuh ah pass down at the Spot later?"

"I had a late night yesterday. I've got to get some rest," Charlie said. He finished his drink. "By the way, Slinga called back."

"Wha' him seh?" D. asked interested.

"He says he's flying in. I'll arrange to pick him up."

"Alright."

Puggy blew out some smoke.

"Who's Slinga?"

"One soldier who used to work with Pablo before dem dip him las' year," D. explained. Checking his watch he said: "I gwan lef' yuh. I want to go pick up my girl before I go Spot."

"Which girl, Sherry?" Charlie asked stretching.

"Nah man, she haffe cool tonight. I promise Jenny fe tek her out."

Puggy got up and they walked downstairs.

"Tomorrow, seen?"

"Alright. Take it easy."

Charlie watched them get inside the car before closing the front door.

He'd only been there once to drop Glenda off, but Linton soon found his bearings. Over the traffic lights, on the left he recognised Manor House Station. Then he took the third right. Glenda's house was the third house on the right, but there was no space to park, so Linton had to push about fifty yards further down. It was 10:42 when he locked the Lexus with the remote alarm. His mobile's shrill ring pierced through the top pocket of his jacket.

"Wait, ah you again? Yeah man, I comin'. I comin' now, jus' cool."

Linton switched off and walked up the road. Phil was a good customer, but too 'hyper'. He'd already called fifteen minutes earlier as Linton was leaving south London. The night was calm, a couple passed on the other side arm in arm. At number five, a dim light filtered through the drawn curtains. Linton opened the low wooden gate and went to ring the bell. A rapid shuffle of feet from inside the house... The door opened. Linton stepped in, brushing past Glenda who held the door open.

"You're early," she said.

The corridor was unlit, the bulb had probably blown. Linton turned, looked at the woman.

"Yeah man, I done my business fast to come check yuh."

Glenda led the way inside the house. The living room was squarish and large with a staircase leading upstairs. Linton sat down on a settee and looked around the room, nodding.

"You live in style, man," he remarked.

It was the first time he had ever really entered her house. Overall the place looked expensively furnished with lots of ornaments. On the thick rug was a nest of smoked glass tables and a blue halo of light from a lamp in the far corner. From the rack under the stairs a stereo unit dispensed a fast techno beat. Glenda had disappeared through the swinging wooden saloon doors into the kitchen. She returned with two glasses.

"So wha'ppen, me ah try fe reach you all week," Linton said.

"I was busy," she said, sitting on the chair opposite him.

"Is why yuh ah wear darkers?" he asked. "De place dark a'ready."

"Oh it's just my eyes, you know."

He didn't.

"You have anything?" she asked urgently, her hands restless on the lap of her short black dress.

"Bwoy, yuh wan' see; I jus' come from south London and de man dem buy me out."

"Oh shit!" she exclaimed, glancing at her watch.

Linton searched through his pockets.

"Me sure seh... see't deh: I know seh me maas one ah dem !"

Linton pulled out a small wrap from his trouser pocket. Glenda got up fast and went through the swing doors again. Linton got up, took a few steps to the open bay windows. A soft wind was blowing the drawn net curtains.

In the garden beyond, a light from the next door kitchen projected a bright circle on the grass. Glenda returned anxious and excited.

"Come on, I've got it."

She sat back down. Slowly, Linton made his way back to the settee.

"Come here man, wha'ppen t'yuh?"

40

Glenda got up and joined him on the settee. He was ready to light up. Glenda glanced at the clock above the entrance.

"Wha'ppen yuh goin' somewhere?"

"No, I'm waiting for a phone call," she answered.

Linton flicked the lighter, the flame rose yellow and blue in the semi-darkness.

"Can I light it?"

She sounded intent on doing it. He let her.

"Sure, gwan man."

Glenda took the pipe, breathed heavily a couple of times before closing her lips around the stem. Flames reflected in her spectacles. She pulled hard as the rock ignited. Then the smoke drifted around her head, thick. Linton smiled, his eyes caught onto something. Under the bright flame, Glenda's brown skin showed two darker spots the size of a penny, puffed up above the watch.

"Ah wha' dis?" Linton asked her.

She blew out smoke, coughed up drily, pulling her arm away.

"Nothing, I burned myself."

She finished smoking and passed the pipe, then got up and went into the kitchen. Linton had smoked a lot with his friends earlier on and didn't feel for anymore right now. He felt cool and relaxed though the music in the room kinda distressed his vibe. He called out:

"Listen nuh, some people ah wait 'pon me!"

She came out of the kitchen, a bottle in her hand.

"Let's have a drink first."

"Nah man, come. We drink later."

Glenda turned around, flashed back in and out of the kitchen.

"Give me a minute," she said, as she crossed the room and ran upstairs. Standing up, Linton lit a cigarette and scratched

41

his head. He wanted to deal with Phil as quickly as possible then get home to have a bath and relax a little bit. He'd been busy all day and needed a rest before going to meet D. at the Spot later on. Now this girl was taking too much of his time. Kissing his teeth, he climbed upstairs after her.

At the top were two bedrooms then the bathroom. Glenda stood in front of the mirror, her back to him, applying make-up.

"Wha' yuh ah deal wid, man? I tell yuh seh me in a hurry."

Glenda quickly picked up her spectacles on the shelf and put them back on.

"I'm coming, I'm coming."

As she turned under the bright lights of the bathroom, the two black marks on her arm caught Linton's eye once again. He was trying to remember where he'd seen marks like these before. The ring of his phone stopped the question on his lips.

"Yeah...? Yuh ah hear me; me deh 'pon me way, seen... Ah wha' de bloodclaat happen t'yuh? Jus' cool, man."

Linton cursed and replaced the phone in his pocket. He felt annoyed that anyone would try to pressure him. As for the girl... He turned around and took the stairs down.

"Hey gal, me gone y'hear? Later!"

Behind him, she called over the bannisters.

"Linton, wait!"

But he was not a man to get distracted from his business, plus he didn't feel quite comfortable in the house. He couldn't quite explain why, but since arriving he had felt like leaving.

The front door wasn't locked. He pulled it open and stepped outside. Walking back down to his car, he called D.'s mobile, but the operator's voice said 'switched off'.

Linton got inside the car and switched on the engine. The familiar sound of reggae music filled the plush interior. He wound his window down.

'Dat idiat gal love freaky music too much', he thought as he brought down the automatic gear lever. As he started out, he saw a car stop near the entrance to the street. It was right in the middle. It would have to pull over to the side for the Lexus to squeeze past. As Linton approached the car, he saw the passenger door open. A man stepped out wearing a ski hat and a shirt. He walked around the front of the car and crossed to the houses on the other side. Linton was already annoyed that the driver blocked his way out. The car, a Renault 5, had its lights on and engine running. Finally the Lexus came almost bumper to bumper with it. Linton kissed his teeth, cursed and sounded his horn, twice, loudly. Pushing his head through the open window he shouted:

"Yaow! Wha' yuh ah deal wid?!"

At the same time to his left, his eye caught a glimpse of something obscured by the tall trees fencing the house next door, until he drew level. The man with the ski hat was half-way up Glenda's front path. As Linton's car horn sounded in the night, he turned his head. In less than a second, his mind cleared of all other concerns. For a man like him, used to the streets and constantly tuned in to the most subtle vibrations, instinct never lied. He saw Glenda in a flash. He couldn't think why, but the two marks on her left arm jolted him. Suddenly he remembered what they were...

They say it all happens in slow motion, but if you think in slow motion, you're not going to make it. For a few seconds after the horn sounded, they were as surprised as he...

In quick sequence, the man with the ski hat pulled something from under his shirt and started running towards the Lexus. Behind him, Linton caught a glimpse of the curtains moving in Glenda's house. He swore and pulled out the gun from his

43

waist.

"Bumbaaclaat, she dead!"

But he realised his life was the one in danger. The driver of the R5 was halfway out of the car now. In his right hand, a black muzzle extended, pointing at Linton. If he deliberated, he was finished. Linton knew that much. He pushed down the safety on his .45 automatic. With his left hand he flung the gear lever into reverse. At the same time he glimpsed to his left the dark holes of a double barrel against his window. Linton literally saw the shots shatter the glass. The noise was deafening. The car lurched back, Linton instinctively pressed the brake as his hands left the wheel and reached up to his face. There was glass in his flesh, it felt like thousands of pins. His hands were wet with blood running down the side of his neck. Yet his mind was still ticking. He reacted in a way that he couldn't have explained rationally. His right hand still held the gun, which it raised automatically, pointing to the left and Linton squeezed the trigger. The first shot was too high, buzzed above the man's head. The other two hit him square in the chest, tearing their way inside. He fell with his shotgun. From the Renault 5, a burst of fire peppered the Lexus' windscreen but it didn't shatter. As Linton pushed the lever to drive and pressed the gas pedal flat, another burst spat out of the sub-machine. This time, as the car lurched forward and collided bumper to bumper with the R5, Linton was hit twice in the chest with what felt like the tip of an iron bar. The other shots got lost skywards as the driver of the R5 was thrown off balance by the force of the impact. Because he was too slow to react, because the Lexus was heavy and already in motion, and because the Renault was a small car, the driver found himself being ploughed backwards at increasing speed.

The pain in Linton's chest was unbearable. He drew in some

air through clenched teeth but kept the gas pedal down to the floor. His brain was still working; he could see the intersection with the main road, approaching beyond the R5. Ten yards to go, five yards... As the Lexus forced the smaller car backwards, Linton took aim through his window, towards the windscreen of the small car.

'Pow, pow! Pow!' went the big gun. The windscreen went down. As the rear of the Renault emerged on the main road, Linton saw the driver's face. It was the same big, red bodyguard he'd faced the night when he and Sticks had raided Simon's club. He was furiously trying to steer the car out of the Lexus' way. Linton let off two more shots, one at least hit home because the driver's face disappeared for a moment.

The Renault was now in the middle of the road. One car coming from the right skidded and managed to swerve onto the kerb. But the van that caught the R5 smack in the middle was coming from the top, going much faster and no amount of braking could stop its course. Linton watched the Renault spin around on impact.

After the terrible sound of metal crushing metal, the night went quiet again. The van driver came out and ran to the assistance of the Renault, Linton turned left and drove off.

Fighting against the deep, burning sensation in his chest, sweat and blood bathing his face, he somehow managed to keep the big car straight. The light at the crossing had just turned red, but Linton didn't have time to stop. He heard the sound of screeching brakes as he zoomed past. He could feel his strength fading. He shook his head, gulped as if to swallow some of the air breezing in from the window. His vision and thoughts were becoming blurred, the muscles in his arms and legs barely obeying commands. Something pulled in his neck. The gun was on the passenger seat, still ready, but Linton knew nobody was chasing. With each turn of the steering wheel his chest felt like someone was twisting a blade inside. If it wasn't for the shit keeping him standing he'd probably have passed out already. Linton winced as the car rolled to a stop. He looked around, feeling feverish now, sweating all over. He unbuttoned his shirt, slowly. The white string vest underneath was dark and wet. He pulled the mobile out of his pocket and glanced around trying to locate his position. Had the phone been in the right pocket it might have been hit by a bullet, Linton considered. Forcing himself to concentrate he dialled D.'s mobile number. It was off...

Breathing in, Linton forced himself to think; he had to call someone before the curtain he felt coming down over him finally fell.

Sweetie... Sweetie, yeah that was it. Hers was one of the numbers he knew by heart, particularly because Bess lived there. Linton dialled the last two digits. One ring... Two rings... Three rings... Silently he thought, 'Come man, answer de phone.' At the fourth ring, a sleepy voice answered.

"Who it is?"

It was Leon, Sweetie's 7-year-old son.

"Leon, ah me, Linton."

"Linton?"

Linton took in some air.

"Listen nuh, whe' Sweetie deh?"

"She's next door, you want me to call her?"

Deep inside his head Linton heard the warning bell. He'd been there before.

"No, no...," he hissed. "Listen yout', tell her... tell her I been shot, seen? Tell her, me deh by Green Lane, near de park... Yuh understan'?"

The youngster was fully awake now. He repeated:

"Yeah, Green Lane, by the park."

"Tell her to tell D..."

At the other end of the line Leon called out:

"Linton... Linton..."

But that was it. Linton had kept up as long as he could. He slumped to the left, over the gun on the passenger seat. He had switched off the engine but the lights of the Lexus were still on. Out of the speakers, a raucous voice was riding a tightly mixed beat, 'Gal Fe Beg'...!

As parties go, this one wasn't too bad. The two young deejays had managed to get the crowd going with the mainly soul-techno mix. Reggae tunes had been far and few between however. To the left of the control desk, D. was sipping some juice, wondering how much longer he felt like staying. It was one thing to be nice and take Jenny to her friend's birthday party, quite another to bear the music they were playing. He checked his watch.

'Another fifteen minutes and I gone to de Spot,' he thought.

Jenny would probably want to stay anyway. He'd come back for her and Carol later. D. eased out of the corner, pushed past the dancers and made his way to the kitchen. Jenny was behind the bar with some friends. She came over.

"You look bored."

D. shrugged.

"Cyaan tek de music."

Jenny laughed.

"You want another drink?"

"Nah man, me alright."

She insisted. "You hungry?"

D. was about to decline the offer when his phone rang.

"Yaow!... Wait I cyan hear."

D. moved away towards the door of the flat where things were relatively quieter. Jenny stood by watching closely.

"Sweetie, what happen? Wha'...?!"

From where she stood, Jenny couldn't hear but noticed right away the change on D.'s face. She watched anxiously as he snapped the phone shut. She met his stony gaze. Then he came back towards her.

"Listen, somet'ing happen. Tek a cab home."

D. was already turning to leave. Jenny had felt the urgency in the tone of his voice, she held on to his arm.

"D., what's wrong?"

He stared at her, his eyes still, his gaze piercing through her.

"Wait for me."

Jenny dived into the kitchen. D. opened the door and stepped out. Jenny came running after him carrying her jacket. D. turned around.

"Yuh stay yah," he said firmly.

He continued walking. Outside, he glanced over his shoulder. Jenny was still behind him. A small group of guests were chatting in the mellow summer night. Carol saw D. rush past her.

"Wait! You leaving already?" she called after.

Then Jenny rushed past her.

"Jen, where you going?"

Still no reply. Frowning, Carol handed her glass to the man she'd been talking with and ran after her sister. She caught up with her just as D. was unlocking the door of his car. Jenny said nothing, simply jumped in the passenger seat. Carol was still asking 'what happen?' but climbed in the back all the same.

D. steered out of parking and gunned the engine, flashing through the back streeets to Wood Green High Road. Jenny glanced at him briefly, his jaw clenched, eyes straight somewhere beyond the windscreen. She knew his thoughts were far away and there was no point in asking questions. Not now, not the vibe he was in.

Carol understood that something serious was up. The shake of her sister's head had told her that she knew nothing either.

With the almost empty early Saturday morning streets, it

took D. less than ten minutes to get to Hackney. He knew the hospital. In a couple more minutes he'd be there.

Sweetie's call had chilled him to the bone. After the first flurry of thoughts he remained icy calm. Only the tension at the corners of his mouth and the narrowing of his eyes gave an indication of how he really felt. Sweetie had only said that Linton had been shot. She and Bess had found him and taken him to the hospital. They were waiting for him.

D. took a hard left, straightened up the car and pushed it down the street at speed. He parked just after the gate, stepped out and started towards the building. Jenny and Carol were right behind him.

The casualty department was having a busy night. Two white men with bandaged heads, one with blood over his mouth sat outside. In the foyer, Sweetie and Bess got up as D. entered. He listened as Sweetie explained how they had found Linton unconscious in his car after Leon had relayed his call. The doctors had taken him into surgery immediately; nothing from them as yet.

Carol and Jenny listened. D. called Sweetie aside.

"Yuh find anyt'ing wid him?" he asked.

"Bess tek dat. What about fe him car?"

D. thought for a moment.

"It can drive?"

"I feel so, but it got shot up," Sweetie said. "Yuh want me move it?" she offered.

"Alright. Tek it to your yard, cover it up. I deal wid it later." D. sighed and nodded. "Which part dem have him?" he asked.

"First floor," Sweetie said.

"You an' Bess go home, I call yuh later."

D. had begun to walk off when Sweetie called. He stopped and turned.

"D., police up deh, yuh know. Me see dem gone up."

D. took in the information.

"Later," he said.

Behind him he heard Jenny's hurried footsteps as she caught up with him. He threw her a glance without stopping.

"Go home man. Dem tings not fe yuh..."

"Like last time..." Jenny countered calmly.

D. didn't answer. He climbed up to the first floor, Jenny and Carol still behind him.

At the desk, a nurse checked on the board behind her.

"He's out of surgery, but you won't be able to talk to him, he's under sedation. Are you his family?"

"He's my brother-in-law," Jenny said, quickly looking at Carol.

"How is he?" Carol asked the nurse.

The woman was young, very calm, professional.

"The surgeon took the two bullets out, but he's lost a lot of blood."

"Thank you," Carol said. "Could we see him, just for a minute?"

"Alright, but very briefly. It's the third room on the left."

"Thank you very much," Carol told the nurse.

The police constable was also young, and visibly bored sitting on a plastic chair beside the door to the room. He got up as D. and the two women approached.

"Hello," Carol said, "can we see him?"

There was a genuine look of concern on her face. D. and Jenny also looked afflicted.

"I'm afraid he's unconscious, are you his wife?" the policeman asked.

"Yes, I'd just like to see him. They drove me here," Carol pleaded as the policeman looked suspiciously at Jenny and especially at D.

"Alright," he conceded finally, "but don't be long."

The visitors entered the still and silent room. On the bed, a tall figure lay still. From above the bed, a drip descended to the left arm of the man. Linton's head was bandaged, a respirator tube connected to his nose. His eyes were closed. On the screen of the machine beside the bed a green line tapped to a regular rhythm. They approached the bed quickly, quietly, D. staring intensely at his friend lying motionless on top. He had spent the whole day with Linton and now there he was a few hours later...

"These things frighten me," said Carol looking at the monitor. Then she looked at D. "He's gonna make it."

D. knew Carol meant it to reassure him a little and sure enough the remark seemed to get him back on track.

"Who shot him?" Jenny whispered.

Despite his own feelings, D. knew Jenny was still affected by that fateful night a few months earlier. Now here it was again. For a time he said nothing, just stared at the bed, shoulders low, standing there like a zombie. The sound of the door opening called him back from his reflections. Slowly he turned halfway. The door closed shut. A man stepped forward and took the few steps up to the foot of the bed. Jenny noticed the look on her husband's face, usually rather inexpressive, transform to pure astonishment. Before she was even sure of what she had seen, D.'s features returned to their usual inscrutable mask. The man greeted the two women in turn.

"Good evening," he said seriously. Then to D: "Wha'ppen Missa D., how is life?"

D. stared at him just long enough...

"Wha' yuh ah do yah?" he asked, not very warmly.

The man smiled.

52

"It's funny; de whole ah ouno ask me de same t'ing. So wha', me cyan come ah Englan' an' mek it like ouno?"

D. didn't see the joke. The atmosphere between the two men was tense enough for Jenny and Carol to feel. The sisters stood quietly there, turning their attention from D. to the man, back to D. With Linton on the bed in the white-walled room, they were both feeling a kind of eeriness. The man was standing in his black suit, white shirt and red tie. He seemed to be the only one relaxed. He must have been in his late thirties, early forties. He had a short beard, stood the same height as D., built a little bigger, squarer. He seemed more dressed for a wedding than for a wake.

"Yuh know somet'ing; I was going to come an' check yuh," the man remarked. D. thought about that briefly. He smirked.

"Check me?" Then he paused and glanced back towards the bed. "So wha', dis is your work?"

Shaking his head, the man grinned.

"You know me bettah dan dat, man," he commented good-natured. "If ah me, him would be at the morgue, not in hospital."

It was as cold as it was meant to be. D. didn't wince.

"So, how come yuh reach here so quick?"

The man moved forward to the foot of the bed, his eyes locked on the monitor.

"Dis is part of my job..."

He sounded almost like a civil servant. D.'s sarcastic tone caused him to turn around.

"So dem finally kick yuh outta de force ah Yard? Now yuh come turn bwoy fe de white man dem."

The man wasn't angry, yet his tone was just that little bit harder.

"Yuh wan' know de trut'? he paused, pointing at D. "You is

de reason why dem send me up yah, yuh know."

D.'s head tilted to the right.

"Me?" he asked.

"Yeah man, you an' de res' ah de lickle criminal dem, whe' jus' run 'way from Yard. Ouno distress de white man dem too much. Dem haffe send fe an' expert fe deal wid ouno." He stressed 'expert' in a proud kinda way.

D. glared at Lancey. He'd never liked him. The detective was the last man he'd expected to see in London. And tonight, the way he felt about Linton, D. could have easily vented his anger on him.

"An' is you, Lancey, dem t'ink seh gwan solve dat?!"

D.'s laugh was bitter, hollow and dropped clearly, sharply in the quiet room.

The man nodded.

"Me hear 'bout you, y'know. Yuh turn big now, get nice clothes, nice car, nice girls too..."

He smiled at Jenny and Carol. They gave him an up and down icy glare. D. turned to his woman, slightly motioned with his head. She nudged her sister and led the way past Lancey, out of the room. The door closed, D. took a deep breath and faced Lancey with an indefinable squint.

"Hear dis now," he began slowly, "when I was a yout' yuh always try fe handle me coarse, an' dem time me jus' haffe run. But yuh see now, I come all the way ah Englan' t'rough money nah run ah Yard."

D. Paused, his voice went a little lower.

" 'Nuff ah we up yah an' me not nuh bettah or nuh worse than anybody. But don't get me wrong; I don't run from no guy. Yuh understan' dat part?"

D. waited. Lancey didn't answer right away, but he understood. At least he nodded.

"I hear yuh, man."

Then he switched to specifics.

"So tell me somet'ing, yuh tryin' to tell me seh yuh don't know who shot your bwoy?"

D. could see his approach. Lancey continued.

" 'Cause dem bring in two more casualties from one shootout tonight, aroun' de same time..."

He left it open, yet D. knew Lancey had made the connection. The police officer left him a couple of seconds to his thoughts, then smiled.

"Yeah man, me see ev'rybody picture a'ready. Me know who ah run what an' where."

It sounded like a little power speech, psychological intimidation. As an aside, he added:

"Yuh know seh me jus' miss yuh when dem lock yuh up ah Yard." Then he paused, glancing at the bed.

"I know yuh wan' de man dem who kill yuh nex' soldier earlier dis year," Lancey sneered insensitively. "Mmmnh, it look like your team get kick out. Wha' yuh ah go do now?"

The door opened, a nurse came in.

"You gentlemen will have to leave now," she ordered the two men, standing in the middle of the room, then checking her watch she adjusted the intravenous tubes connected to the unconscious patient.

"More drugs," Lancey said wrily, looking at the drip.

The nurse left. D. had had enough for the night. He cast a long glance at Linton lying with the plastic tube in his arm. Without a word to Lancey he turned and walked to the door. He knew Lancey would want to get a last word in. He was right.

"Remember, D.; I am de new sheriff," Lancey said lightheartedly. Then he added on a more serious note, though not quite threatening:

"One mistake an' yuh gone."

D. turned before closing the door on the unwelcome encounter.

"Yeah, yuh watch me..."

In the corridor, the policeman was still in his chair. As he walked back towards the desk, D. saw two more uniforms further down the corridor but didn't pay them no mind. Jenny and Carol were sitting beside the lift. They went down together and out of the hospital building. D. led the way to the car, events spinning in his head. Meeting Lancey after all this time and especially tonight, had left him with a bitter taste. He reviewed the whole situation, assessed his position and pondered what his next move should be. Behind him, Jenny and Carol talked in barely audible whispers. They climbed inside the car.

It took almost ten minutes of driving, but eventually Jenny asked:

"What's going on, D.?"

He felt edgy, but he had to be cool for now. It was no use taking it out on Jenny.

"Don't worry 'bout dat, I deal wid it," he answered calmly.

But Jenny couldn't help worrying. She had to offload the stress she was feeling.

"Don't worry? Linton is fighting for his life, there's a policeman from Jamaica after you, and you tell me not to worry?"

D. turned to her.

"Watcha now; don't get involve, seen? Dat is my business."

Jenny stood his look then turned away. At the back, Carol kept quiet. Jenny stared through the windscreen at the road ahead. D. heard her quiet remark.

"It is your business. But when your friends start dying 'round you, how am I supposed to feel?'"

He had nothing to say. He needed to keep his mind clear, now more than ever.

D. pulled over in front of Carol's house. He turned to Jenny.

"I need to see Charlie, I'll pick you up later."

Carol got out and said good night. Before stepping out, Jenny put a hand on her husband's arm, squeezed it.

"You need some rest, don't be too long."

The remark sounded incongruous but D. knew what she meant. He glanced at his wife, slipped the car into gear and drove out as soon as she had slammed the door shut. Jenny stood momentarily on the pavement, following the car's rear lights as they disappeared into the night. Then she went inside.

Somehow the music didn't sound sweet tonight. D. switched off the stereo. Doing barely 60 in the near-empty High Road, he had no real desire to stop driving. So he ignored the right turn that would have taken him to Camden and pushed straight up, attracted by the road ahead. He was in no great hurry to tell Charlie the bad news. What could he do now? Coasting easily with the Audi in 4th gear, D. flashed through Highbury and drove all the way down Upper Street, turning left at the Angel almost against his will. He could have driven like that without ever stopping. A few minutes later he somehow found himself in Shoreditch. Yet as he parked he knew why he was there. He hadn't been to check the house for almost a week. Picking the right keys out of the bunch, D. made his way inside.

The light was working which meant there was still juice in the meter. The house was cool, silent but for the low buzzing of the fridge-freezer in the kitchen from which D. picked up a bottle of water before making his way into the living room. Everything was as Donna had left it. One of Cindy's hairpins was still lying on the music centre, where it had been abandoned in the last minute rush before the drive to the airport. Since they'd flown out, D. had only been there occasionally. He sometimes passed by in the day but had only slept there two nights in the last few weeks. Usually he stayed in Leyton whenever he wasn't by Jenny, which had been rare lately.

D. kicked off his shoes and sat on the carpeted floor, the bottle of water between his folded legs. His back against the settee, he scanned the familiar surroundings of Donna's living room. Only the light in the passage was on, D. liked it better that way. He sat motionless for what seemed like a long time, eyes open, unable to erase the spiral of thoughts that kept dragging him back to the same point. Tonight, D. felt something he had not experienced in a long time: helplessness. He tried looking ahead, weighing up all the options dispassionately, but one fact was inescapable and whatever he did, nothing could make it right. He realised that things would never be the same. He would never again get that buzz he had at the beginning. Sticks was gone, Linton was barely alive and that was that. Now he was forced to play a hand, whichever one, but in the end he knew he'd never again feel as carefree as he had when he first set up the business. The phone on the little table in the passage prompted another line of thought. D. remembered that he had not called this week, despite all his earlier promises. He tried to dismiss the idea; he was in a crisis, this was not the time to worry about women... But the phone kept beckoning him... reminding him. Maybe that's what he needed to do, lift up the phone and call. At least that part of his life was still there, that mattered...

D. got up, picked up the phone and placed it between his feet. He sipped some more water then dialled, quickly calculating the time difference. In Jamaica it was still evening, around 9.30pm. They should still be up. Sure enough, two rings only and a voice came through from the other side of the ocean:

"Hello, hello?"

D. cleared his throat.

"Hallo, who dat, Cindy?"

"Yes, who is it?"

"Cindy, ah me, man."

"D? Hi D., how you doing?"

D. felt good to hear the little girl, she sounded all grown up.

"Where is yuh sista?"

Avril was sleeping, she had busy days.

"Which part yuh madda deh?"

"She's on the veranda, hold on..."

Cindy had left the phone hanging to run get her mother. Shortly after, someone picked up at ther other end. D. could still hear Cindy's voice in the background.

"Mummy, tell him..."

"D., what happen?"

He recognised Donna's voice instantly.

"Notin' How yuh stay?"

"Me alright. How yuh nevah phone back since?"

"I talk to Leroy this week still."

"Leroy? But yuh fe call me, man. What happen, yuh nah miss me?"

"Yeah man, me miss yuh, y'know."

As he spoke, D. realised he meant it.

"Which part yuh deh?" Donna asked.

"Me deh home, ina de livin' room."

"So how yuh sound so, man?"

"How yuh mean, me sound 'so'?"

59

But his voice couldn't lie to her.

"Yuh sound like yuh far."

"Me far, yes..."

"Nah man, not like dat. I mean, like yuh 'ave t'ings on yuh mind."

D. sighed, tried to sound a little more relaxed.

"Me alright, man. Jus' tired. Y'know."

"Yuh bettah get some sleep. So yuh eat today?"

"Yeah man, me eat."

"Which part yuh eat?" Donna insisted on knowing.

"Down by GB, man."

"Ohhh," she said simply.

"So how Avril?"

Donna laughed.

"She... she ah mad woman. Yuh wan' see her; she get rude, yuh see."

D. smiled as Donna explained how his daughter was beloved by every one in the area because of her antics. They all said she looked just like her father. He felt good to hear that.

"So, how de business go?" D asked.

Donna told him of the progress she and Leroy were making. By the following day, she said, all the paper should be ready for the land deal at the solicitors. D. asked a few more questions then Donna concluded:

"We gwan work it out, D. Me nevah know me miss Jamaica so much. Life too miserable in Englan', man. We haffe come an' set up yahso, soon. D., yuh ah hear me?"

"Yeah man, fe real."

D. answered more quietly than he should have.

"Me put on some weight, yuh see man," Donna said.

D. said she shouldn't worry about that, he didn't mind.

"So yuh gwan keep me even if me get fat?" Donna asked laughing.

"Yeah man, me nuh matter dat."

They talked a little more, finally D. promised he'd call by Thursday to find out if all was going as planned.

"I miss yuh, y'know," Donna said down the line.

"Yuh soon see me, Donna."

"Yuh mus' tek care, y'hear? 'Member say yuh have family."

Somewhere inside, D. felt that. Donna had given him something that he could use on a night like tonight. It was as if she knew.

"True, an' me love dem." He paused. "I gone now, seen. I will call Thursday."

He heard Donna's farewell then replaced the receiver.

He remained in the same position, dozing until the early morning sun lit up the living room.

I warned you, didn't I? No shootings on my patch."

"Yeah, I know... Something went wrong..."

"Too right, something went wrong! 'Cause you're a fuckin' head case, that's why!"

"Look, I need some time..."

"You keep it up an' you're gonna get a lot of time, you know what I mean? Look I've got to go, see you later. Same time, same place. Don't be late..."

The line went dead.

"Fuck you!" Simon shouted, slamming down the receiver. He would have liked to tell him to his face, that fucking cop! He hated the man down to his wise-cracking tone of voice.

'What the fuck is happening?' Simon asked himself for the hundreth time. He had not slept, could not eat, could think of nothing else but the desperate situation he was in. How come it had all gone wrong? Getting up, he paced the living room to the garden window at the back then returned, hands in his pockets, cursing and muttering to himself.

"I musn't let the pressure get to me," he repeated to himself several times.

Finally he sat himself down on a chair, trying hard to focus and trying to think his way out of the problem. The bright sun squeezed its rays through the half-closed blinds. The antique clock near the large, potted cheese plant read 11.10. It could have been much later for all Simon knew, he had lost all notion of time since Glenda's midnight call. The girl was sobbing, almost hysterical at the end of the line. Once Simon made sense of what she was saying, it felt like the ground was moving beneath his feet. And that idiot crying down the phone, asking him to come meet her at her mother's house. She had to be crazy. Simon swore at her, told her to stay put and not to call him again. The whole thing was a shambles.

"That fuckin' girl," Simon muttered under his breath. His rage was mainly directed at Glenda. She was the cause of all this. He had set up the perfect plan, how it had failed was beyond his understanding. Following the call he split quickly from Julie's house without a word, ignoring her questions. First he drove around to clear his mind, driving on and on with no particular place to go until he ended up at home. From there he tried to locate Cole, but his mobile was off. Simon gave up trying to find him, he had probably heard about the shooting anyway.

All Simon could make out from Glenda's call was that there had been a gunfight outside the house and that she had fled before the police got there. She was too freaked out to answer his questions, but even without the details it was clear that everything had gone disastrously wrong. On the big desk in the adjoining room he used as an office, looking on to the garden, a mound of white powder stood out against the black, glossy wooden top. He'd spent most of the night since reaching home sitting at the desk, getting wrecked. One line, one sip of brandy, one line... By the time dawn surprised him, Simon had no idea how much stuff he had snorted. It was out of character for him to do so much in one go, he was no junkie. Yet tonight he'd have taken anything to rise above the vile taste of it all. He was no wiser after the binge, however. At best he dozed off for an hour or so, stretched out on the sofa. The unwelcome ring of his phone had woken him, calling him back to the ugly reality. And then it was that cop.

Simon ignored the insidious beckoning of the white stuff across the room and made it to the kitchen. He gulped down the last quarter of juice in the fridge. The click of the key inside the street door lock alerted him suddenly.

"Simon!"

He stepped out of the kitchen.

He and Cole met in the corridor. Cole took off his glasses.

"What happened?" he asked.

"I don't know what the fuck happened."

Simon walked into the living room.

"Where you been, man?"

Cole followed him.

"I went by Lucy and crashed out. Thursday night was heavy man..."

"Who told you?" Simon asked.

"The kids on the estate all know some shooting went down. I just come from there." Cole shook his head and sat down.

"Our 'friend' just called me," Simon said.

Cole looked at him, waiting.

"One dead, one in intensive care."

"Who's dead?" Cole asked, eyes wide.

Standing by the TV, Simon sighed.

"Chico."

"Chico!" Cole's voice echoed, unbelieving.

Simon pressed the TV button.

"Yeah, Chico..."

"Oh shit!!!"

Cole bowed his head slightly forward as if searching the carpet in front of him. But he found no explanation there. He said nothing for a while. The news was heavy to digest. He knew Simon was thinking the same thing. Finally he said it, low.

"You shouldn't have let him go."

Simon didn't need to hear that. He knew already. He started

pacing again.

"I know that, but you saw him. He was crazy that kid. He wanted to be a gangster..."

He paused.

"But what went wrong man, I mean how?" Cole asked.

"How the fuck should I know?" Simon started. He stopped abruptly. "Oh shit!" Something in his mind, a sudden idea. "That fuckin' girl..."

Cole guessed.

"Glenda, yeah where is she?"

"She called me, crying and all that. She says she don't know what happened. The shooting happened outside."

Simon shook his head. Cole was trying to work it out.

"She was supposed to keep him in, right? Chico was taking the back, Butch was the one to do it..."

Simon was still pacing.

"A perfect plan, fucked up!" he raged.

"Is the guy dead?" Cole asked.

Simon shook his head then flopped into a chair.

"Shit!" Cole said, almost despite himself. Then he sighed heavily. "You think she gave them up?"

The question had been on Simon's mind but he was ahead of his sidekick.

"Whether she did or not, she knows everything. If the police shake her up a little, she'll give us up."

Cole knew what Simon was thinking. He leaned back in the chair, put his head back wearily.

"It's all got to stop somewhere."

"What are you saying?" Simon asked.

Cole turned his head towards him.

"It's gotta stop, or it's gonna fuck up the whole thing."

"You think I like shootings?! I'm a businessman, this is

hurting me."

Simon was edgy. The whole thing sounded like a nightmare, only he was in it and he was awake, wide awake.

"So what d'you want to do next?" Cole asked somberly.

"Next?" Simon repeated. He looked rough, not his usually dapper self with his clothes crumpled, his eyes shady, unshaven. The situation was sudden and disastrous but Simon was trying to hold on to a thread, something to feel positive about.

"Alright, we got hit, but we're almost there..."

He paused, realising that Cole wasn't following him.

"...We've got to hold on until at least the end of the year. After that, we'll have enough to start operating above board. By then, the gym will be finished."

It sounded fine, Simon had it all planned like clockwork. He knew how long he'd have to continue drawing cash from the street and how he would switch to the legal schemes he'd set up with bank loans, how he would progress in the promotion game and earn himself large percentages. He didn't seem able to see what Cole was trying to show him.

"What about Butch, Simon man. What about Chico?" Cole asked calmly.

The thought of future plans had lifted him up but with Cole's reminder Simon's face reverted to its glum countenance.

"I know, I know..."

He got up, slowly walked to the door and leaned against the frame.

"They're gonna come after us. You know that," Cole stated matter-of-factly.

Simon looked at his friend, frowning. Cole continued.

"You know it, these guys don't play. We killed a couple of them and they've got more guns. We can't take them all."

Simon listened, but somehow he didn't share that opinion.

"What you talking about? They're the ones who tried to take over. We're defending our turf, remember?"

"Yeah, I remember... But they're not going to stop. They're gonna keep coming."

Simon raised his arms.

"So? We've got the weapons, we've got the people. This is ours."

Cole didn't answer. He could see Simon was tired and upset. "Look, we've got to pass by the estate, I won't be long."

Simon disappeared into the bathroom for the next twenty minutes.

Cole stared at the TV but couldn't get into the sports programme. His head felt empty, filled with a dense smog. He rubbed a hand across his face. Without being pessimistic he still didn't find anything positive to think about, unlike Simon. It wasn't the shooting in itself. He had willingly done his bit to avenge the original insult to Simon. But he felt bad about last night's hit.

Simon had been furious when he realised that Glenda had been 'turned'. He found out soon enough; the girl was too hooked on stuff not to arouse suspicions. Sure enough, under pressure she cracked easily. If she hadn't, Cole knew Simon was prepared to continue burning her skin with acid until she did. The plan was brilliant, almost like one of those 50's spy thrillers. Unfortunately it had all failed but Simon still couldn't see certain things as clearly as Cole.

They left, Simon looking a little fresher, though he insisted on doing a couple of lines before departing. They climbed inside Cole's Toyota and joined the Upper Street traffic, windows down to let in the mellow air. Saturday afternoon shoppers milled around on the kerbs, the pace was leisurely, anything to stay outside in the sun. Cole drove sharply in the traffic, picking the gaps, sunroof open, his eyes alert behind the shades. Simon pulled an envelope out of his pouch and checked the contents, counting carefully. He caught Cole eyeing a wad.

"I'll be glad to see the back of this greedy fucker."

He slipped the envelope back in the pouch, lit a cigarette.

At the estate, they parked near the shops. On a fourth-floor landing, a group of young children rolled carefree over on the concrete, their mothers leaning over the balcony walls chatting. Simon and Cole went left, stopping by the second door. It took a few knocks, but eventually the panel opened and a lanky blonde-haired woman, blinking against the oblique sun ray, welcomed the two men in.

Dressed in washed-out jeans, the woman had a kind of wet smile. She avoided looking directly at Cole and Simon as she ambled back to the bare living room muttering something. She turned, smiled at Simon out of washed-out blue eyes.

"How is it going, Si, alright?"

Simon said he was fine. A little girl emerged from inside the flat, a few biscuits carefully clasped in her hands.

"Mum, I'm going out," she said.

Her mother muttered again, avoiding Cole's stare.

"All gone?" Simon asked her finally.

"Yeah, yeah."

"Well, what you waiting for?"

The woman couldn't have been more than thirty, a couple of years either way, but at close quarters her face seemed older. She laughed nervously and stepped out of the room. Cole glanced around furtively. There wasn't much to look at. The place always smelled bad also. The woman shuffled back in and handed Simon a brown paper bag with another shaky smile.

"It's all there, I don't need to count?"

The woman shrugged. Hands waving in the air, she said:

"No, well, not all. You see, the kid was sick... and I took some to buy the prescription. I was going to put it back later and..."

Simon held up his hand, stopped the flow of explanations.

"How much?"

She hesitated.

"How much?" he asked again.

"One twenty." she said finally.

"One twenty?!" Simon repeated glaring at her. "You smoked that shot yourself, didn't you?"

"No, no. I..." she protested.

Simon came closer.

"I told you before; don't slip."

The woman's hands were already shielding her thin face.

"Honest Simon, I wouldn't lie to you..."

Simon knew she was lying. She was cracked out, but there were too many bigger things to deal with today. He shook his head, pointed a threatening finger at her.

"You better pay it back."

He pushed the paper bag in his back pocket. The woman was adamant.

"I'll pay it back, don't worry. You know how it is, Simon."

She followed them to the door.

"I'll send one of the kids," Simon said over his shoulder as he stepped out into the light.

The door closed behind them. The two men made their way downstairs.

"That bitch is fucked up, I ain't gonna give her nothing more," Simon insisted as they crossed the road towards the shops.

"Then we need someone else to deal on the estate," Cole

remarked.

"That shouldn't be too hard to find."

Simon stopped abruptly.

"What the...!"

The sentence was left unfinished. The man sitting on the bonnet of Cole's car, seemingly absorbed in his newspaper, looked all too familiar.

"Shit!" Simon grunted between clenched teeth.

The man seemed to notice them only when they stood in front of him. He looked up.

"How you doin'?" he asked smiling.

Cole and Simon remained unsmiling.

Strangely enough Simon found himself wondering how the man could be wearing a jacket and tie in this heat.

"What do you want?" he asked curtly.

The man folded his newspaper carefully.

"You don't look happy to see me, we need to talk."

Cole was watching him behind his glasses. Simon frowned; the last thing he needed today was this kind of surprise visit. The man stood up, started towards the pool hall. They had no choice but to follow. Inside, a dozen boisterous youngsters gathered around the machines, surrounded by the deafening sounds of a radio station. The man headed for the back room, walking in on a handful of youths busy around the pool table.

"Everybody out!" he announced loudly.

They all stood there, looking shocked by the intrusion. They took in the man's dress and the look on his face and then they saw Simon looking gloomy behind him. Wisely, the youths decided to quickly fade out.

Lancey pulled the curtain across the door frame. Relaxed, he picked up one of the cues abandoned upright against the table. Cole and Simon stood on the other side of the table by the wall.

They watched the man line up a shot. The white ball sped across the baize and hit the number '6' spot. It went down with a clang. Lancey didn't look up, but walked instead to the short side slowly, lined up again. He straightened up and picked up the piece of chalk on the side.

"Yuh know, I nevah know there was so much excitement in dis town."

It was a matter-of-fact tone, he didn't even look at Simon. Once he was satisfied his cue was properly chalked up, Lancey leaned over the polished wood edge, took aim and struck the white. The crash of the number '2' going down startled Simon. The man was making him nervous. He sunk one more ball. Now there was only one spot left. Simon couldn't tell whether he missed it on purpose. Lancey stood up and smiled.

"Your play."

Simon really didn't feel for any kind of game today. He knew the man was testing his cool. Their eyes met.

"Your play man!" Lancey insisted.

Simon sighed and picked up the other cue. From beyond the curtain the bounce of a rhythm floated in. Simon blew out some air, took aim trying to concentrate. The ball only slightly missed the pocket.

"Unlucky!" Lancey offered, from across the table.

He finished the game quickly, sinking the black ball hard. Simon put down his cue.

"So your boys messed up last night," Lancey remarked casually, while finishing Simon's play.

"I don't know what you're talking about," Simon said drily.

Lancey looked up at him. He was sitting on the edge of the table facing him.

"It look like yuh love playin' games, y'know. I told yuh las' time: I know everyt'ing dat goes down 'round yah."

"Look man, I don't know what you think you know, that's nothing to do with me. So why don't you just leave me alone, I've got things to do."

That Simon had made a bad move was evident. Lancey waited a little, as if reflecting on something. Simon didn't like the pause. He was becoming positively edgy.

"You know what I think?" Lancey started, "I think you're afraid, now that your people start getting shot..."

"I don't give a fuck what you think," Simon retorted angrily. He didn't appreciate being taunted like that.

Lancey shook his head, looking down. He looked back up at Simon and grinned.

"Oooh, so you're a bad bwoy."

Then the grin was gone.

Fast, too fast for Simon to see it anyway, Lancey raised the cue he still held in his hand and smashed the big end onto the side of Simon's neck. At the same time he was on him, his left hand around Simon's throat, stifling his cry of pain. Lancey stood him up against the wall. He had seen Cole's move almost before it started. Lancey's left foot kicked into the air and slammed hard into Cole's stomach. Then he yanked Simon as if he was a rag doll and threw him onto his friend, sending them both crashing to the floor. With one hand, Lancey grabbed hold of Cole and pulled him upright. His right hand patted his waist, pulled out the gun. The policeman looked at it briefly, then without warning smashed it into Cole's face. The glasses flew off, broken.

"Yuh wan' play big man game?"

Cole's mouth was bleeding. Lancey let go of his shirt collar, and slapped him across the face with the back of his free hand. Cole slumped to the ground, groaning. Simon remained motionless on the floor. Lancey yanked him by the collar and stood him up. His eyes inches away from Simon's, deep, dark and merciless. No more smiles...

"First of all, yuh bettah learn to show some respeck when yuh talk to police."

Lancey pushed the gun's muzzle into Simon's neck. Simon breathed heavily, unable to back away. He could hear Cole retching on the floor.

"Alright, alright!" he cried, the throb in the side of his neck burning, spreading right through the shoulder. He heard the click of the safety on the gun, tensed up, braced himself.

"I don't t'ink yuh tek me serious, y'know," Lancey told him.

The gun pushed deeper into Simon's neck.

"Aaargh!"

Cole was struggling to sit up straight. Lancey looked down at him.

"Yuh comin' wid me; assault on a police officer," he said in a serious voice. "An' concealed weapon too," he added, then turned back to Simon. "Didn't I tell yuh I was de new sheriff?"

Simon couldn't see the joke. His head was hot, buzzing with pain. He didn't know if he was supposed to answer. He decided against it.

Lancey looked at him and released the pressure on the gun, a little.

"So, why yuh order de shootin'?"

The voice was calm. Simon was no fool, this man was very serious. He breathed in deeply.

"I have a score to settle."

Lancey's laugh wasn't merry, just sarcastic.

"Settle? Listen lickle bwoy, yuh don't settle nothin'. I tol' yuh, I deal wid your problems."

He paused and sneered.

"Your two bwoys couldn't even deal wid one ah dem. Dem

73

man too rough fe yuh. Yuh should know dat."

Cole stood up slowly, holding his stomach. Lancey glanced at him.

"Which part yuh get de gun?" he asked.

Cole looked up, didn't answer. Lancey kicked him in the leg. Cole cried out. Lancey kissed his teeth, lowered the gun and pulled Simon by the collar.

"I'm going to take you both in, we need to talk some more."

"Look officer, we can work out something. No need to take us in."

It was Cole who had spoken through his pain. He knew they wouldn't be welcome at the station. And Simon did too. Lancey looked at Cole, then at Simon — held tight in his grip.

"What is he sayin'?"

"He's right, let's talk," Simon said.

"Yuh bettah talk fast."

Lancey patted Simon down quickly and felt the bulge in his pocket.

"Wha' dis?" Eyes trained on his captive, Lancey took out the paper bag. Simon said nothing. Lancey let him go and perched himself up on the edge of the pool table, scanning the contents of the bag.

"Yuh full ah cash, bwoy."

The grin spread across his features. He turned to Cole who was propped up against the wall a few yards away. Then Lancey laid the black gun down on the polished wood beside him.

"I have to confiscate dis. But I'm gonna give yuh a chance..."

Simon felt his neck gently, his eyes on Lancey and the bag.

"That's business money," he said weakly.

"Yeah, business," Lancey smirked. "Crime pay it look like."

Cole pleaded.

"Look, we can negotiate. We're only small, you don't want us."

Lancey looked at him almost kindly.

"You know somet'ing, yuh sound like somebody sensible." He turned to Simon. "Why should you tek all de heat? I don't want to come back to yuh all de while and pressure yuh. Is bes' we understan' each other."

"Okay," Simon agreed. He would have agreed to anything at that moment. The man terrified him.

"Dis is how dis t'ing works," Lancey announced, pushing the paper bag inside his jacket pocket. "I tek care ah yuh enemies. You stay cool."

He got up, picked up the gun and clicked on the safety. "I check yuh every weekend for my fee."

Lancey paused, looked at Simon, straight-faced.

"Any questions?"

Simon shook his head.

"No, no questions."

Lancey tucked the gun in his waist behind him.

"Good," he added. "And remember, this is strickly confidential. You keep quiet. Yuh understsan'?"

Simon nodded, he understood very well. Very cool, Lancey picked up the cue from the floor and placed it carefully on the green. Then he adjusted his jacket and straightened his tie.

"So, later. Have a nice weekend."

With that Lancey walked out leaving the two men propped against the wall, shaken. For a minute or so the music from next door was the only sound in the room.

"That cunt robbed us," Simon declared finally, massaging his aching neck.

Cole winced from the pain in his gut. He wiped his mouth with the back of his hand. Simon was in pain too; feeling angry

75

at the whole thing. Not only had he lost some money, but he felt humiliated, low. Yet he could do absolutely nothing about it. He was trapped and he knew it. He remembered something, looked at his watch and swore.

"Still have to go and pay the other one now."

The situation seemed absurd. Deep inside, Simon knew he couldn't win. They had him and were going to keep squeezing him from both sides. Lancey had made it clear that he wasn't to tell anyone about their arrangement so he would simply have to find the cash to keep them both happy. Simon reminded himself that he only had to keep it up for six more months or so. He had set himself that target and he had to make it. One thought kept dancing through his throbbing head.

'I have to get out of this'.

With a groan, Cole bent down and picked up his broken sunglasses.

A week and a half after the shooting, Linton was still in intensive care. His was what doctors described as a 'serious but stable' condition. They told Sweetie and Bess — who visited the hospital everyday — that he'd been hit on the left side of the face. If he made it he would need surgery to repair the damage. The police guard had been removed after a few days. D. had arranged to have Linton's car moved and kept in a safe place. Things on the street had been calm all week, but there was an expectant atmosphere, everyone watching. Even the police were watching, D. knew that. Because of their network of informants they knew when something was up. The man at the centre of things was presently at home, a brooding look on his face, listening to arguments he knew were valid but to him seemed nevertheless secondary.

"...And especially now man, cause you're the target. They're all watching you. You've got to give it time. "

D. said nothing for a while. 'Time', he thought, 'I don't have no time'.

"So what about respeck, Charlie, respeck?" Puggy asked.

D. looked at the young singer. That was exactly the point. How come Charlie couldn't see it.

"Respect? I'm down with respect, but you make any move now and you're playing in their hands. Respect has got to wait."

The meeting had been going on for a good few hours. Charlie could see D.'s point but was the only one who really insisted that the time wasn't right. He knew there had to be a payback, but not now. It was too dangerous...

"Charlie, yuh hear me?" D. started. "We cyaan wait; if we don't revenge de bredrin dem, de man deh 'pon street cyan look up to me again. And if we don't cut dem down now, we lost de territory. Simple as dat."

Charlie knew D. was right, yet he said:

"If you move now, police is down on you. Plus that motherfucker Lancey, man."

Though Charlie didn't know Lancey, D.'s description of the man had painted a grim picture. His arrival on the scene couldn't have been more badly timed. Charlie weighed up the situation for a long time before telling D. to expect the worst. He understood that Lancey wasn't playing by any rules. Around the room the core of D.'s crew, which didn't amount to many people, had gathered. Pablo was there, sipping on a beer and selecting cassettes for the stereo. Occasionally he checked on the TV where some European football was on. He wasn't talkative tonight; Linton's shooting had upset him and he had already made his position clear. The guilty should be made to pay now, tonight if possible. To his right, Costa sat, burning a spliff and listening to the exchange. Though he was a late addition to the team, he played a major part in managing the Spot for D. who had not forgotten his quick thinking on the night of Sticks' murder. To his right, next to D., was the returning 'veteran' Slinga, whom D. had now installed in Linton's room. He'd arrived two days before from the States where he'd spent the past six months. After being deported from England, Slinga had managed to find his way to California where his older brother had set up a base. He looked a litle bigger, but still had that inscrutable face. He had listened in silence as Charlie and D. argued their points, aware that a crisis was on.

"Lancey bettah keep 'way from my runnings, cause I not gwine skin up wid him." D. paused. "Yuh see him, as a yout' him used to persecute me, y'know. Him woulda kill me when I beat up him breddah. But by then I was with Skeets an' Lancey nevah wan' cross him."

Slinga spoke up for the first time.

"Dat police deh wicked, man."

"Fe real," Pablo agreed, "him kill 'nuff people ah Yard."

"Any bwoy try tek 'way my living," D. declared, sounding very determined, "done wid, yuh know dat. I don't care who him is."

Charlie could see he was the only one urging caution. He didn't insist, though he had a bad feeling about the whole thing. But what could he do? He could see both sides of the argument, yet knew D. couldn't change his attitude. On the street your soldiers have to know you always stand by them. They take the risks and get things done so that your plan works and money rolls in. The moment anyone feels you're not a hundred percent, everything starts to crack at the seams. D. had started reorganising his team. He turned to Pablo.

"From today you takin' over Linton's job. Everyt'ing 'pon street, the lab, the collection... ah your business dat."

Pablo nodded.

"I tek care ah evert'ing, don. Don't worry yuhself."

"Me still ah work wid Pablo, right?" Puggy asked from his corner.

"Nah man, I want you off de streets."

"Wha' yuh ah deal wid, don? Yuh know seh me haffe involve."

D. shook his head. It had been hard to keep Puggy down since Sticks' death.

"You should concentrate 'pon de music, yuh know rude bwoy. Charlie don't want yuh get mash up out deh."

Charlie didn't. He shot his artist a disapproving glance. Puggy frowned.

"I have to mek some money an' music business slow, yuh nuh see't?"

He had a point. D. looked at Charlie, then turned to Puggy. "Alright, hear wha', you stay down ah de Spot wid Costa."

It was better than nothing, Puggy concluded. D. trusted Costa to keep the impulsive youth under control. Pablo inserted a brand new cassette in the stereo unit. The voice of the operator boomed out, defiant and loud. Then a furious beat crashed through. A tough track with a raw mix. Pablo was impressed.

"Which part dat record?" he asked Slinga.

"Texas."

Pablo listened to the string of lyrics flowing in perfect sync with the drop. What sounded like a roar of human voices drowned out the music.

"Comin' like a million people dung deh," Puggy remarked,

" 'Nuff Yard man deh ah Texas?" Pablo enquired.

"Excess amount," Slinga replied, nodding. "Dem ah run t'ings now."

"Yeah man, me 'ave coupla cousins down deh," Costa added. "Big time operations ah gwan."

D. noticed Charlie observing him thoughtfully. They had been talking about the States a lot lately. Charlie was all for trying to set up a base over there where, he said, money was faster. D. was still considering the options but insisted on clearing up the problems in London first.

Costa and Pablo were still discussing the scene in the States, stressing the fact that Jamaicans had succeeded in carving a sizeable amount of the trade for themselves.

"Yard man 'ave high profile in the States, y'know. Ev'ryday dem ah call fe we name," Slinga said with a little grin.

Pablo smirked.

"Same so dem ah gwan over yah now, ah talk 'bout we tek over."

"Tek over, yes," Slinga added. "Yardman nah run from no guy."

D. looked at him and picked up his bottle of beer. Slinga's return strengthened his hand. The youth seemed more determined than ever in a way and D. needed that extra boost for the work ahead. Puggy started recounting some stories of his tour in the States the previous year. D motioned to Slinga next to him.

"My yout', yuh check out de position?"

"Comin' like de business under attack, don," Slinga answered.

That was a fair assessment of the situation, D. paused then asked him:

"How yuh woulda play dis?"

It was a big question and Slinga felt it. Only his eyes moved, fixed on a spot at the other end of the room for a moment, then back to D. After a few more seconds he spoke, slowly.

"If a man work fe somet'ing him haffe keep it. Anybody try diss de programme we jus' remove him."

That was exactly the way D. felt. He didn't need to ask any further.

Slinga continued.

"An' yuh see de bwoy dem whe' kill Sticks an' shoot Linton, me personally wan' deal wid dem an' wipe out dem whole family. Me vex 'bout dat, y'know don."

"Me know, man. Like how yuh reach now, we gwan deal wid de matter."

"Rewind, rewind man!" Puggy called out.

The taped session was hot with several major MCs and new lyrics from all of them. Pablo obliged and everyone got the opportunity to again check out the stinging arguments the MC was delivering at speed. A little after that D. told Slinga:

"Listen rude bwoy; you get de toughest job. I gwan put yuh in charge of security. Yuh report directly to me. Yuh response fe my personal security."

Slinga listened. He looked straight at D. and said simply:

"I got your back, don. Yuh safe."

No more needed to be said, Slinga knew his job. Around 11pm, Costa got up and took leave. He was on his way to the Spot. Puggy said he'd be down later. First he wanted to reach a shebeen in south London where he'd been the previous weekend. Since he could get a change for a stint on the mike , he decided the move was worth it.

"Don, yuh nuh wan' check out de place?"

D. said maybe. Charlie was unsure and said something about his pregnant wife. D. smiled at him.

"Yuh cyan help her again, yuh done de job a'ready."

The soldiers laughed, Charlie too. Eventually they decided to drive down to the shebeen, for a little while at least. Around one o'clock everyone moved out, Pablo with Puggy in his car, Slinga following D. and Charlie at the rear of the convoy. The night was sweet, warm with a breeze.

"Why is he driving so fast?" Charlie asked, slowing down to stop at a traffic light near Liverpool Street. Pablo had zoomed past the red.

"A good getaway driver dat," D. chuckled.

"So when you gettin' your car, man?" Charlie asked.

"I suppose to go fe it Friday."

D. had been waiting two weeks for his new transport. A friend Sammy had found him a nice, almost new BMW 5 series at a good price. He was customising it for D. a little. Charlie geared up the car as they approached London Bridge. A police motorbike was parked at the kerb, where an unfortunate driver was being questioned. The crew saw Pablo's car parked further up, waiting for them. Ten minutes later they approached the neighbourhood where the shebeen was and parked on the other side of an estate near Old Kent Road. Quite a few people were hanging around parked vehicles talking and drinking. The boom of the bass located the house. In front, a few couples and some rude boys cooled out. Judging by the smoke and heat that rushed out as the front door opened, inside was definitely hot. Behind a table, two men sat casually, a third man leaned against a wall. D. took out a £20 note and dropped it on the table.

"Five ah we, seen?" he said, drawing the attention of the fat gate man with his back to the wall and stepping into the smoky interior, but the man had eased off the wall and now stood in front of D. With the noise level, it was impossible to hear what he was saying. Slinga — who was coming behind — didn't bother asking the man to repeat himself. Swiftly, the youth flashed past Charlie before anyone reacted. D. had not moved, but simply stood staring at the man. He felt someone brush by him. The next thing he knew Slinga was steaming into the gate man — pushing him against the wall, one hand tearing at his shirt.

"Wha' yuh ah deal wid? Yuh crazy?" Slinga asked the startled gate man.

The two men at the table got up but Pablo told them firmly to remain seated and calm. D. touched Slinga.

"Let him go, man."

Reluctantly Slinga obliged, keeping his eyes on the man. One of the other two muttered something to D. and shook his head. Everyone cooled off once the misunderstanding was straightened out.

"Him mek a mistake, him nevah recognise me," D. told Slinga.

Far from excusing him, Slinga pointed to the man.

"Yuh bettah learn people faces, bwoy; 'bout yuh wan' search the don...!"

Eventually they stepped inside, Pablo making a way to the room at the back where the set had strung up. The right corner of the room, under the window, was the best spot. The crew settled there, got some drinks and chilled for a while, taking in the rapid succession of recent releases. The selector knew his job well; not too much chat, just warm up his crowd a little, then kick the start a couple of times. A circle of rude girls in the centre were setting the dancing pace, demonstrating various styles with application.

D. emptied half a bottle of beer and built himself a spliff. He was right against the back wall, Charlie to his right, a window to his left. In front of him, Pablo and Slinga were keeping time to the music, bogling easy. Slinga had once confided to D. that he used to be a selector on a little disco in his original area. In any case he could dance! Sure enough a couple of the girls in the centre had begun a discreet progression towards the two soldiers. D. lit up his sensi spliff, exhaled long, moving to the beat. He opened up his shirt a little, bathed in the sheer human heat of the room. He felt calm despite the pressure of the last few months. In fact the pressure had been on since the beginning of the year.

'Pure bad vibes...' D. thought, taking another deep draw of the cool herb. He suddenly realised that he'd been back in London less than a year, yet he had not had much time to stop and reflect. Looking at it now, he'd been having a rough time. With a little touch of justified paranoia, D. was thinking, 'It look like de whole ah dem ah give me a fight'. Then he drifted

84

into another thought. 'Dem wan' see me broke...'

Physically D. was in the dance, familiar with every record the selector flung down, and rocking. But inside his head the thoughts chased each other. Thoughts of now, thoughts of yesterday... He recalled how he felt when he first settled in London. Though he didn't really know the English scene in the beginning, when he checked it out it was the same all over anyhow. The hustlings, the danger, the enemies, the very same scene everywhere. To his right Charlie said something. D. leaned over a little.

"You want another drink?" Charlie repeated.

The bottle was nearing its end.

"Yeah man, nice."

After all, D. didn't mind letting himself go a little tonight. If he got home red it didn't matter. Since his return from Jamaica he had been pretty straight, working hard. Never too much to drink, a reasonable amount of good herb but strictly no stock. He wondered a little how he'd been strong enough to resist the temptation. He couldn't quite figure it out but he was still straight. There had to be something strong inside him, he thought pleasurably.

The drink arrived. The selector had the two rooms shaking. Around 3 or 4am were often the best times for a session. By that point, everyone was in tune to the collective height. Puggy had been gone for some time. D. could see him now just behind the selector, head bowed, listening attentively to the rhythm, looking for some specific angle to work off. Puggy had musical skills and came up with perfectly constructed lyrics at a moment's notice. He was still a little wild in character but when it came to music, he could work over and over at a vibe until he felt satisfied that it was the best. Charlie had been coaching him in this way, to give his best always. He knew the youth had huge potential. Lately he had gotten Puggy to record several straight swingbeat songs, convinced that he could break into the US market. Right now Charlie was casually observing his protege. Even the short, well-proportioned girl that had been hanging by his side couldn't distract him.

D. lit up his spliff again. He felt more detached now. He was still very aware of the crisis on his hands but not worried. Something in the atmosphere tonight reminded him of those nights at High Noon early on. Next to him Charlie was sipping his drink, watching Puggy as he took the mike. With his usual bravado the singer teased his audience before touching down on the 'Sleng Teng' rhythm remixed '94 style. The selector had to ease up the needle and play it forward. Puggy gradually got to the dancers. By the time he hit them with the third song, simulated gunshots saluted his performance. He had that feel for the crowd which meant that he always knew what type of lyrics to sing, when and where. The crowd shouted their approval. Charlie had a satisfied grin on his face.

"This youth's gonna blow up!" he shouted to D. over the noise level.

A little while after, D. and Charlie stepped outside to let the cool night air revive them. Inside, the smoke alone was heavy, never mind the heat. Sitting on the bonnet of his car, Charlie stretched.

"I'm glad I don't go out regular no more, but this set's playing nice."

D. agreed that the vibe was sweet.

"By the way, you hear from Sweetie today?" Charlie asked.

D. said he hadn't spoken to her in two days.

Charlie yawned.

"You going back down? 'Cause I wanna go home and sleep. I've had it for now."

D. shrugged.

"I gwan move as well."

They saw Slinga on the porch, cooling out by himself, taking in the scene. Charlie motioned towards him.

"He takes his job seriously. That's good."

D. nodded.

"Him is a serious yout'."

"Yeah, he asked me to get him something, you know..."

"Him need a tool, yes."

Charlie corrected.

"He says he needs two..."

"Two?"

"Yeah, two nines, preferably Glock, he said."

D. smiled.

"Me ah tell yuh seh him serious, Charlie."

D. and Charlie hung outside a little longer but by 4.30am they were both ready and headed home across the river to their sleep and another day...

There was no parking in sight. They had been once around already but all the spaces in the small car park were taken. On the High Street an army of traffic wardens on the go forbade any attempts to try there. Finally a middle-aged, white couple turned into the car park and walked to their car. At last. Sweetie geared up and entered the park, positioning herself ready to occupy the soon-to-be-vacant spot. The couple left, Sweetie backed in. On the passenger seat beside her, Bess was still silent, apparently nodding to the rhythm of the music. But Sweetie knew she didn't really hear it. She was always silent for a while after leaving the hospital. They had been going to Linton's bedside every day, usually in the morning. Bess would touch his hand and pray, as if convinced that it would somehow bring the man back from his coma.

'No change', the nurse had said.

Bess and Sweetie had gotten to know her. A young calm and polite nurse who never tired in giving them hope. Sweetie didn't like hospitals. She felt uncomfortable, eager to get out. Today they went to visit Linton early, in order to take care of the Saturday shopping right after. Whoever spoke of 'hotter than July' must have meant it, because today the heat was sweltering. A mid-July weather such as this in England was the exception rather than the rule. Since early June, the sun had been an almost daily feature. The weather man was already talking about the lowest rainfall in years. Sweetie locked the doors, she and Bess made their way to join the multitudes on Kingsland High Street. At the centre of things in the area, the market was sure to be packed on a Saturday morning, especially with a tropical weather such as this. The trick was to reach early, buy quick and get out again, before the bulk of the shoppers invaded. Some didn't even really come to shop; but simply couldn't resist the opportunity for a good gossip with friends in the midst of the jostling crowds. It was still not 10 o'clock, yet the market was already thick with people.

The two women stopped by the jewellers first, where Sweetie had a repair to pick up. Then the heat was on; pushing, shoving, sidestepping... After an hour-long improvised gymnastics through the lengths of the stalls and back, picking up food as they went, the two women ended up back by the traffic lights facing the supermarket, laden with two bags each, beads of sweat curling on their foreheads, in the middle of a noisy mass of people eager to cross over.

"Come man," Sweetie told Bess.

They crossed and progressed alongside the High Road. They were halfway to the car park when someone called Bess' name loudly from across the road.

"Bess! Yaow Bess!"

At the same time a voluminous woman made her way through the traffic jam, squeezing past the bumpers. They stopped, waiting for her to reach.

"Ah you me ah look for. What happen?"

"Wait! Mitzy! Wha' ah gwan?" Bess smiled.

Mitzy greeted Sweetie, but it was Bess she wanted to talk to.

"Me ah wait 'pon yuh, y'know. You did tell me Thursday."

Now Bess remembered what she had forgotten. Straight-faced she said:

"Hear wha'ppen; me did change de pattern y'know."

"Change de pattern?!"

Mitzy had entrusted Bess, about two weeks earlier, with the design of a suit for an important occasion. Since she was rather big built and extremely fashion conscious, she wanted something special. That wasn't really a technical problem for Bess, a talented and qualified clothes designer, she had simply forgotten to finish the suit.

"Yeah man. Yuh see like how me did set it before? Well, I do a different top, yuh understan'...?"

Bess proceeded to describe the modification and its advantages.

"But Bess man, yuh sure dat will look good 'pon me?"

Mitzy seemed worried. Bess looked at her surprised.

"Ah wha' yuh ah seh, Mitzy? Ah new style dat. Trust me, man."

"De christening is tomorrow, y'know."

Bess didn't flinch.

89

"Yeah man, me know. But yuh nah go till late."

Mitzy smiled.

"I have my outfit for the church an' t'ing, but dat suit is for de party later. Me haffe trash!"

"A'right, check me ah yard. In de mornin'," Bess told her.

" 'Bout what time?"

"Around uhm... two o'clock. Alright?"

Mitzy said that was cool, took leave and crossed back over to rejoin her friends across the road.

Bess and Sweetie picked up their bags and continued until they finally got to the car, relieved to lay their burden down.

"Ah so Englan' hot?" Bess said climbing into the car.

Sweetie wound down the window and started out of parking. She manoeuvered expertly to penetrate the bumper to bumper line on the High Street.

"Yuh bettah enjoy it, 'cause when dat place get col', it bad man."

"Colder dan Canada?"

"No man. Notin' colder dan Canada."

Sweetie laughed. Bess could handle the English cold in that case. She had moved to Toronto aged 5. At that time Sweetie had already lived there for a while. When she left, Bess was still a young girl but had kept in contact and finally ended up with her in London. Except for her older brother, the rest of Bess' family was still in Canada.

The women made it home finally, where an insistent bassline greeted them from upstairs.

"Dat bwoy crazy!" Sweetie exclaimed. She shouted up the stairs a couple of times.

"Leon! Leon!"

There was no sign that her son had heard the call. Sweetie shook her head and went for the broom behind the kitchen door. A few vigorous knocks on the ceiling got the desired results.

The volume of the music went down. Upstairs the sound of a door swinging open was followed by the syncopated rhythm of feet coming down the stairs two by two. A slim boy with an innocent face appeared at the kitchen doorway.

"Hi Ma, I didn't hear you get back."

Sweetie turned to her son, disapproving.

"How yuh fe hear me; yuh ah run dance up deh!"

Leon smiled mischievously. He was almost 8 now and had arrived from Canada with Bess, to live with his mother now that he was too big for the aunt who had raised him. Although he knew Jamaica and regularly spent holidays there he was much more used to Canadian life. After being in London only a couple of weeks, Leon had declared that this was a small town and complained that there was nothing to do. Accustomed as he was to skyscrapers, wide roads and big cars, he felt strange at first. Within the next couple of months however, he met youngsters in the area and got acquainted with his new surroundings. Things really weren't that different, he discovered.

"Yuh get your breakfast?" Sweetie asked her son.

"Yes Ma."

"Alright, dis is wha' yuh gwan do: wash your hands, tek de onions an' tomatoes..."

Sweetie proceeded to direct her son on how to start the cooking. She'd realised to her dismay that he knew very little about cooking, apart from the odd omelette. He'd been used to burgers and frozen, microwave-heated food. Sweetie had decided to change his focus and train him. As she had told Bess:

"Dat way him don't have to depend 'pon woman."

91

Leon was learning fast. He was a good boy really, a little mischievous, but not rude. Sweetie was very proud of him. She also had a little girl living back in Jamaica with her mother. She missed her, but while wanting to bring the child over she knew it was best she should begin school in Jamaica where education was still in the old style.

"I gwan set up the dinner, then we gwan check Charlie," Sweetie told Bess.

She soon took over from Leon; after all she intended to eat today...

Once dinner was ready, Sweetie and Bess left again to make some moves. Leon was already back to his music. The traffic through Holloway was thick. Camden was worse. Eventually Sweetie parked and they walked up to Charlie's house. Marcus was in the front garden, playing with two other boys. He stopped just long enough to kiss the two women. The door was open. Sweetie rang the bell and they walked in. Charmaine came out of the kitchen.

"Mornin' missus," Sweetie said.

Bess greeted Charmaine.

The three women decided to sit on the balcony. Charmaine brought out some cold juice. They chatted a while. The sun was bright, the sky cloudless.

"So how yuh feel?" Sweetie asked Charmaine.

"Not too bad now. I'm out of the morning sickness."

Charmaine didn't look that big yet but the heat made her feel tired more quickly.

"You having a girl this time?" Bess asked.

"I hope so. I don't want another rough boy like Marcus."

They laughed. Marcus was a handful, everyone knew that.

"So what Charlie want?" Sweetie asked.

Charmaine kissed her teeth.

"He wants another boy, can you believe it?"

About the same time, they heard a noise upstairs and shortly after, a pair of naked legs appeared coming down the stairs.

Bare-chested and in his shorts, Charlie was scratching the back of his head. He mumbled something in answer to the greetings from Sweetie and Bess.

"How yuh can sleep ina de heat, man?" Sweetie remarked.

Charlie paused before entering the kitchen.

"I had to catch up on some rest."

Charmaine threw Sweetie a knowing look.

"He raved last night..."

"So your wife expecting an' yuh ah rave?"

"Just cool, Sweetie. Don't even start her up."

Charlie knew his cousin well enough; she could trigger an argument he didn't need. Charmaine had been edgy and irritable enough in the last few weeks.

"So how de nursery business ah go?" Bess asked.

"Slowly, but we're making progress. Jenny's supposed to pick me up later to go to a meeting," Charmaine said.

They had started a community nursery project together with a few other women. Charmaine explained that they were getting a council grant soon, once the transaction for the building they had chosen was completed. Charlie and D. had provided the money for the deposit on the building.

"Charlie, don't go back to sleep. I wan' see yuh," Sweetie called out, as Charlie climbed back up the stairs, a carton of juice in one hand. He laughed.

"Come on up."

Sweetie left Bess and Charmaine and followed him upstairs. On her return down, she and Bess took their leave. Downstairs Sweetie gave Marcus a pound coin, told him to be good.

"Bye, Auntie!" he grinned.

There were no short cuts back to Hackney, they had to join the slow moving flow of vehicles. On the radio, one of the two stations involved in the promotion of the Rasta Festival was doing some heavy plugging. A host of artists were due to appear, most of the major sound systems in the capital had booked in, plus some from country. The following weekend was sure to be busy. Sweetie had co-ordinated the organisation of the stores and supplies and other logistics, for the artists were all performing for free. Like the radio deejay was saying, it was bound to be a "bombastic" festival.

Sweetie pulled over in front of a house in Stoke Newington and tried the bell but no one was in.

"Pam must have gone shopping," Sweetie said, as she climbed back in the car beside her friend and drove down towards Clapton. Sweetie slowed down past GBs. On the side of the road, across from the restaurant, a tall man with shades was leaning casually against the bookie shop wall reading a newspaper. Sweetie stopped the car.

"Norris!" she called. The man looked up. The two women climbed out of their car and crossed over.

"Wha'ppen, yuh lose again?" Sweetie teased him. Norris smiled.

"Nah man, me jus' put down somet'ing. I cyan lose today."

He sounded sure.

"Hear wha', me ah look fe one gal whe' usually hang 'round yah..." Sweetie began. She described the girl. Norris tried to figure out who she meant.

"Yeah man, yuh see her before. Alright, 'member one time me see yuh comin' outta GBs an' one gal beg yuh ah money, yuh brush her off."

"Oh dat gal? Yeah man." Norris recalled the girl. "Lyn... ah one crackhead gal, man," he added. "Wha' yuh want wid her?"

"Is somet'ing me wan' ask her 'bout somebody. Yuh know where she live?"

Norris didn't know. Though he was listening to Sweetie, he had been admiring Bess, staring her down through his glasses. Bess just stood there, cool.

"So what happen baby?" Norris addressed her finally. "Yuh lookin' sweet today."

She was. In fact Bess was probably one of the most attractive women around. With her rich brown complexion, almond-shaped dark eyes and naturally curly, long black hair, very few men could help feeling attracted to the young woman. She also happend to have a fine, slim but shapely figure. Norris had all but forgotten about the horses.

"What about yesterday?" Bess asked mischievously.

"Every day, man, me ah watch yuh all de while. To tell yuh de trut' yuh is de crissest woman 'bout yah; fe real."

Norris already had one hand on Bess' arm. She watched him with a knowing smile. She was used to Norris trying a thing on her.

"Except for Pearl, nuh true?!" she countered.

That was a trick question. Norris' girlfriend wouldn't like to learn that he found Bess more attractive than herself.

Norris sighed.

"How yuh ah gwan so Bess, man?"

Sweetie cut in.

"Norris, yuh bettah go back to your horses dem. So, yuh don't know which part I could find de girl?"

Norris shook his head.

"Ask the cabbie dem," he offered. "Maybe dem know."

Sweetie thanked him.

"Come Bess, mek we check it out."

"Later, Norris. Hol' it down," Bess told the man.

95

He watched her walk across the road before returning to studying the racing forecast in his paper. Sweetie drove down to the mini cab office a little further down. Bess stayed in the car while the older woman went to investigate. She came back a few minutes later and stood on the pavement while a young African driver gave her directions to the woman's home.

"De yout' seh she live off Clapton Park, in one ah dem tower blocks."

They drove down and stopped by the shopping area. A group of youngsters were hanging around outside an off-licence, taking in the sun and the loud beat from a ghetto blaster. Sweetie called one of them over and questioned him. After consulting with his friends, the youth returned.

"Yeah that's the same girl, she lives on the seventh floor in that block," he pointed.

"What's her name again?" Bess asked him.

"Lyn."

They thanked the youth and walked across to the flat. The lift smelt dank, its floor partially wet. The women emerged on the seventh floor landing, revived by the fresh air.

" 'Round yah nasty," Bess said, blowing air through her nostrils.

The youth had said that it was the first door on the left out of the lift. Sweetie knocked hard on the wooden panel. No answer. Three more loud knocks before some noise fliltered out from inside the flat.

"Who is it?" a voice asked defensively.

Someone was peeping through the spyhole. Sweetie and Bess exchanged glances.

"Lyn, open up, man!"

Bess spoke as if she knew the girl.

"I don't know you," the voice replied.

96

Sweetie had a sudden thought.

"Look, Roy gave us something for you," she said. "But since you're messing about, forget it."

She motioned to Bess and they walked away, not too far. The girl was bound to know Roy, a local dealer. Sure enough, almost immediately the door was unlocked from inside; it opened with a squeak.

"Wait, wait. What's happening?"

A red-skinned, short girl was standing by the door. Strands of hair stuck out from underneath the baseball cap. She had on a white vest and faded jeans cut at the knees.

"What's happening? It looks like you're hiding from somebody," Bess said, as she and Sweetie turned back towards the flat. They simply walked inside, past the puzzled girl. She closed the door behind her visitors and turned to face them. She couldn't have been older than 25, with tired eyes and drained features. She stood nervously, arms by her side. On the couch, a baby boy of around a year old had just stopped crying. When he saw the two visitors, he started again.

"Shut up!" Lyn yelled at him. She turned to Sweetie and Bess. "Roy sent something...?" she asked with a poor smile.

"Yeah man," Sweetie said.

Sunlight bathed the living room. Apart from the couch, there was a narrow, broken wall unit against one side. A few children's toys and an ashtray were strewn on the floor. Bess went to the couch and gently picked up the little boy. He wore a dirty T-shirt and his nappy, judging by the smell, was soiled.

"Him need changing," Bess told the girl. "Bring a diaper."

Obviously the child wasn't a priority for Lyn. She simply stared at Sweetie, more interested in what Roy had supposedly sent for her. Eventually she walked away down the passage and returned quickly with a clean nappy. Bess took it and started to change the little boy, went to the kitchen for some water and tissue.

"Look nuh, Roy said you could help us. We're looking for a girl."

"What girl?"

Lyn had her arms crossed over her thin chest.

"Glenda. Yuh know her, ain't it?"

Lyn made an effort, searching her muddled brain.

"No, I don't know..."

"Yuh know her, man. A brown-skin chiney gal. She works in a club. Roy said you're related to her."

Puggy had been the only one able to describe the girl, after that Sweetie had asked around and she came up with Lyn as a possible connection to get to the woman. Lyn's washed-out face lit up briefly.

"Oh Shirley! Yeah, she's my cousin."

So the girl had another name...

"What do you want her for?" Lyn asked.

Bess had finished changing the little boy. He seemed more relaxed now but was still looking curiously at the two women.

"How old is your son?" Bess asked.

"He's one... almost," Lyn said, glancing at the little boy.

"We've got a job for her," Sweetie explained. "But she's not at home. You know where to contact her?"

Whether Lyn knew or not, her mind was elsewhere.

"What about Roy?"

That was it, that was the real interest for her. Bess sat the child back on the settee, he didn't cry. Then she turned to Lyn.

"Listen, do you know where your cousin is or not? We don't have no time to play. You understand?"

Lyn was taken aback by Bess' suddenly aggressive tone. She recoiled, as if expecting violence.

"No, no. I don't know nothing."

"Hold on, hold on..." Sweetie said to Bess. She turned to Lyn.

"Alright, look; Roy said you could help. You tell us, and I give you this."

Out of her pocket, Sweetie pulled out a small piece of foil paper. Lyn's reaction was immediate. She uncrossed her arms, her eyes opened up. She stepped forward, one hand already outstreched.

"Wait!" Sweetie closed her hand quickly. "Tell me where Shirley is first."

Now Lyn's brain was working fast, trying her best to unravel information in her head. Her eyes kept straying towards Sweetie's closed right hand.

"Shirley, she's not at home... Her mother, she must be by her mother's."

Bess was looking at her, unsmilingly. Lyn sounded sure, she wanted to be sure.

"Where she live?" Sweetie asked.

"Just down by the station."

"Which station?"

"East Ham station."

"You're sure?" Bess asked the girl.

Lyn nodded.

"If she's not at home, she's gotta be there."

"Alright," Sweetie said, "East Ham. But which road? You know the road?"

Lyn was getting a little nervous, she scratched her head through the cap.

"I don't know... I can't remember."

Bess looked at Sweetie; she thought of something. Lyn's eyes were still fixed intensely on Sweetie's closed hand.

"Yuh need some shit, right?" Bess asked the woman.

99

The response was rapid, unhesitating.

"Yeah, yeah, I need some."

"Okay, we're gonna give you some."

Lyn looked bad but her eyes lit up.

"This is what you're gonna do for us. I want you to call Glenda... Shirley, and give her a message. Okay?"

"Yeah, okay. I'll call."

At that precise moment Lyn would have sworn to do anythinig Bess asked her to. Whatever she had to give in exchange for what was in Sweetie's hand didn't matter. Bess looked at Sweetie. If Glenda's mother had a phone they wouldn't have to go there; they would make Lyn bring the girl to them.

"What's the phone number?" Bess asked.

"I've got it somewhere."

Bess turned to Sweetie, "Give her the stuff, man."

Sweetie stretched out her hand and in a flash Lyn grabbed the small foil paper and disappeared into the kitchen.

"All we have to do is set her up to call the girl, tell her we've got some shit for her. She will come," Bess reassured Sweetie. Sweetie nodded and smiled at the plan.

"Yeah man, but not now, next week," she said.

Bess wondered why the delay.

"We have this one now, she will do anything fe we," Sweetie told her.

That was true. The little boy started moaning again. Bess picked him up and soothed him gently. Lyn came out of the kitchen — the smell of crack all over her. A transformation had occured on her face. She looked almost normal.

"Alright?" Sweetie asked her.

"Yeah, thanks."

Then Lyn remembered the deal.

"I'll call her."

"Not now, we're setting up the job first. Next week we come back to see you, then we'll call her together, yeah?"

"Yeah, yeah. No problem."

"And I'll get some more stuff for you," Sweetie added.

A smile appeared on Lyn's face.

"Alright, thanks. What's your name?"

"Sharon," Sweetie told her.

"You better feed this baby here. He lookes hungry," Bess said, handing Lyn the child. She looked phased out but took hold of him nevertheless.

"Alright, we'll be back next week."

"Yeah, when?"

"One evening next week, man. Make sure you're here."

"I'll be here. I'll be here."

Sweetie and Bess left the girl and her child and took the lift back downstairs.

"Dat gal sick, man," Sweetie said once they were back on the street.

"Yuh should have seen the kitchen, rat must be in deh. Me sorry fe the baby," Bess shook her head.

They climbed in the car and headed home to their awaiting dinner.

The wipers set on the first position cleared the windscreen easily of the drizzle, but it started to fall heavier. It was the first serious rain for over three weeks. Each night the TV weather man talked about 'the drought' and the natives longed for relief from the sweltering heat that had England seeming like some Caribbean outpost. There it was, pouring down now, sending people rushing for cover. D. switched the wipers to a higher speed as fat drops of rainwater fell crashing onto the windscreen. Next to him, Slinga was his usual laconic self. Even in the wet conditions, the car was a dream. It responded perfectly, smoothly around the curves, steady on the straight. D. had picked it up from Sammy's garage on the previous Friday. Since Sammy had gotten him the deal, D. had been only too pleased to give him a neat little commission. With tinted windows, polished alloyed wheels, rear spoiler and all-leather interior, the BMW 525i was the business. Sammy had it resprayed green, D.'s favourite colour; not bright but a deep emerald green. D. shifted down into second and flashed past the lights at Turnpike Lane station just before it hit red. A light touch on the brakes and the big car eased up noiselessly. Even when the stereo was turned down low you could hardly hear the engine.

It was still full daylight, just after 7pm. But the grey clouds above would turn day into night earlier than usual. Sherry usually finished at this time on Wednesdays, as far as D. could remember. He hadn't seen her in over a week and had decided to surprise her. He turned left before the shopping centre and found space a little way down the street as a car was pulling out. He parked and switched off. The rain gave no sign of abating. It was just as well that he'd taken an umbrella along when he'd left home earlier on.

"I soon come," D. told Slinga.

He opened the door, unfolded the brolly and stepped out into the downpour. It wasn't cold at all, just very wet. D. made his way to the hairdresser's salon. He got there just as Sherry and a friend were about to leave. The friend saw him first and nudged Sherry.

"Oh hi, Tony!" Sherry exclaimed, stepping quickly outside. She joined him under the umbrella. "You nearly missed me."

D. smiled.

"I have good timing."

Sherry's friend was a little way off under her own umbrella. She was tall, with brown skin, pretty enough.

"You know Maxine?" Sherry asked D.

He'd seen her a couple of times before when he'd picked Sherry up. The two girls were best friends or something.

"Yeah man, yuh a'right, Maxine?"

The girl smiled and said she was fine.

"Can we give her a lift, she lives in Seven Sisters?"

D. said that it was cool and the three of them hurried down to the car, sheltering.

"Is that your new car?" Sherry asked excitedly as they approached the gleaming 5-series.

"Yuh like it?" D. asked proudly.

He let the two girls in the back. The umbrellas went in the boot, to avoid wetting up the interior. The rain was easing up slowly.

"This is my bredrin, Thomas." D. introduced Slinga.

Sherry and Maxine said 'hello', Slinga glanced back and answered in kind. D. drove off, getting back on the main road.

"When did you get it?" Sherry asked, admiring the luxurious inside of the vehicle.

"Las' week."

"It must have been expensive?"

"I got a good deal," D. said casually.

Maxine looked around wide-eyed, almost intimidated to be inside.

"Yuh have a new hair style," D. said, admiring Sherry's newly-plaited hair with wavy extensions that framed her dark, attractive features.

"I got it done yesterday, do you like it?"

"Yeah man."

Slinga turned around and gave Maxine a penetrating look.

"Yuh ah hairdresser too?" he asked

"Yes."

Slinga said nothing more for a while.

"So wha', yuh hungry?" D. asked Sherry.

"Yeah, kinda..." she said.

"What yuh feel for?"

Sherry wasn't sure, she thought about it.

"Chinese?" she asked after a while.

"Bwoy, me nah too deal wid Chinese, y'know. Too much pork."

"Oh yeah."

Sherry remembered D.'s dietary restrictions. He usually took her to dinner during the week when he came for her. They also went out at weekends sometimes, not always. D. had been seeing Sherry regularly since they had met again at his New Year's dance. D. liked the way Sherry was, discreet, not fussy and sensible. He found her quite mature mentally. And she in return enjoyed every minute he could spend with her. She wasn't interested in him for status or glamour, or even plainly for the money as many girls her age are. Sherry didn't really think like that. She learned a lot with D. and always had fun.

"Maxine, yuh wan' come have dinner?" D. asked.

Maxine hesitated. Sherry turned to her friend, smiling. Maxine often told her she was lucky. She wasn't envious, just happy that her friend had a 'glamorous' man as she called D.

"Go on Max, come along, you're hungry ain't you?" Sherry encouraged her.

Slinga turned around again.

"What happen, yuh madda waitin' fe yuh?"

It wasn't the nicest way to motivate a woman, but it worked.

"No, I don't live with my mother," Maxine stated firmly.

Unwillingly, she had just given away a little private information. D. glanced briefly at his lieutenant.

"So what yuh feel to eat?" he asked the girl.

Again Maxine hesitated. Sherry sold her out.

"She likes Greek food."

"Greek?!" D. repeated, trying to figure out what type of food that was.

Maxine defended her tastes.

"Yes, Greek. You never had Greek food before?"

"No, yuh know. What dem eat?"

Maxine proceeded to describe what Greek cuisine consisted of. It didn't sound too bad. D. said he'd try it. Slinga said nothing. Eventually Maxine directed D. to a restaurant she'd been to once and they ended up in Harringay.

The rain had stopped now, dusk was slowly descending on the city. D. parked not too far from a brightly-lit restaurant with a white facade. They made their way in and were directed to a table by an eager waiter. The menu was explicit. They all ordered what they wanted. It was still early and only two of the other tables were occupied. In the background, some stringed instruments etched a plaintive melody. Slinga had been looking around the room, observing everything in his silent way. He was seated next to Maxine, opposite D.

The food arrived finally and they all set to deal with it. A few more patrons had come in, the waiter seated them efficiently.

"Did you sort out your problems?" Sherry asked D.

The last time she'd seen him he had seemed preocccupied, in a sombre mood. Sherry didn't usually ask him about his business. She knew more or less what he was involved in, but she never brought it up. She'd heard about Linton being shot, like many other people in the area. One of Sherry's older cousins was also a hustler. On one occasion, she'd arranged for him to get a deal from D. or rather, from one of his soldiers.

D. swallowed some food and nodded.

"Everyt'ing under control," he said.

As far as possible he tried to keep Sherry away from the problems associated with his business. That was a separate part of his life. Yet she sometimes followed him on his moves and had been to the Spot with him a few times; she probably knew more than he thought she did. Danger didn't phase her, neither did guns or the police. She had told D. at the beginning that her father had done some time in jail for possession and supply of ganja. That was when her mother left him.

On the other side of the table, Slinga and Maxine had struck up some form of conversation. He had got her talking and she answered his questions but still seemed a little distant. She wasn't exactly shy but maybe used to a different kind of date. D. watched them while eating, amused. Sherry noticed that.

"Has Thomas just arrrived, then?" she asked D.

"Nah man, him come up before."

"He doesn't smile much."

D. knew that to anyone who didn't know him, Slinga seemed

a little cold most of the time. The waiter came up, smiling politely.

"Is everything alright?"

"Yeah man, nice," D. said.

"Would you like dessert, coffee?"

Nobody wanted any. The waiter left and returned shortly after with the bill. Slinga stretched. D. turned to Sherry.

"What time yuh goin' home?"

She shrugged.

"Anytime, mum's working nights."

Sherry's mother was a nurse but in any case she wasn't strict and Sherry did pretty much as she pleased.

"Yuh want to go movies?"

D. liked going to the movies. As a youngster he'd frequented the local cinemas on Spanish Town Road quite regularly, sometimes venturing all the way to Crossroads to catch the latest Kung Fu or Western. His favourites were still adventure movies. Sherry said she'd been meaning to go and see the latest Wesley Snipes film. D could relate to that. Sherry turned to D.

"You know something: you look a little like Wesley."

Given that he was her favourite actor, it was a compliment. D. laughed.

"G'way wid dat!"

"No, seriously, you do, except..."

"Except wha'?"

"The eyebrows."

D. couldn't see what she meant, but then again...

"Anyway, is him try look like me," D. concluded.

Sherry laughed.

"Maybe you could become an actor."

It sounded intresting.

"Me can act y'know," D. said.

Opposite them, Maxine presented a challenge for Slinga. He was apparently trying to get through to her, talking low, about something with which she didn't agree. But he had the arguments, and he fired them in his rapid patois leaving Maxine asking him to repeat himself. Sherry cut in.

"Maxine, you wanna go pictures?"

The food had relaxed Maxine, she was more forward now.

"I should go home, you know. I didn't plan on staying out."

Slinga looked at her and grinned.

"Relax Maxine, man, you getting entertained tonight. Yuh safe."

Maxine didn't comment on whether she felt 'safe' or not. After a quizzical look at Slinga, she asked Sherry:

"What are you going to see?"

Sherry opened her eyes wide.

"Wesley..."

"Wesley?! Oh alright then."

Apparently Maxine also had a fancy for the handsome actor. The matter was settled. D. paid the bill and they returned to the car, headed for the cinema in Turnpike Lane.

There wasn't much of a queue outside. Inside was cool and dark, the previews already showing on the large screen. They sat a little way from the back, the two women side by side, D. and Slinga at either end. The movie started, action-packed. The plot wasn't bad, D. was enjoying it, with Sherry snuggled up beside him. Halfway through, a whisper of voices called his attention to Maxine and Slinga on the other side. Someone in a seat behind said, "Shhhh!" Maxine turnd to Sherry and whispered something in her ear.

"Wha'ppen?" D. asked Sherry.

She laughed.

"Maxine says Thomas is too fresh. D. smiled and got back to

the movie. They left shortly after the film ended. On the way out, D. noticed that Maxine kept a distance from Slinga. Back in the car, D. turned to the back where Slinga had slipped in beside Maxine. Smiling, he teased the girl.

"Yuh mus' control yuhself, yuh know sis. Not in de movie house."

Maxine didn't find it funny.

"Your friend's too rude," she told D.

He could well imagine that.

"How yuh ah gwan so stush, man?" Slinga asked, unperturbed.

They drove out. At the back, a low-volume discussion was going on.

"Yuh have some business to do?" Sherry asked D.

He shook his head.

"Notin' special. I'll pass by de Spot later on."

Sherry leaned back in the leather seat, let the music sink in. She'd been waiting over a week for D. to come for her, now she was in no hurry to get home. Maxine however, had to be dropped off. Slinga climbed out to walk the girl to her door. Apparently, he had made up some ground and stayed a little while talking to her in the doorway. He climbed back inside the car. D. drove down to the Spot to drop him off.

"Tell Costa I soon come," D. told him.

Then he headed home with Sherry.

Thursday and Friday, clouds kept swallowing the sun. The light shower on Saturday morning lasted only an hour and by the afternoon, a clear blue sky over Clapham Common welcomed the thousands arriving for the first day of the two-day event.

Everything had been organised 'to the max' so it all went well. The talent show kicked off around 3 pm; contestants of all ages and styles presented their stuff to the highly-receptive and colourful audience. The dozens of stalls spread in a wide semicircle at the back, facing the stage, were well-furnished. The engineers had worked practically all night to set up the PA stystem and they had done a brillant job. The bass pumped in a 3-mile radius from the stage, throughout south-west London. Needless to say, the police had deployed their forces at strategic points but the packed crowd — which covered the vast expanse between the stage and the stalls — was uniform-free. By the end of the afternoon, when a bemused and diminutive 7-year-old girl was declared winner of the talent contest the atmosphere in the park was electric, warm and convivial. Everyone went home high and happy.

From daybreak Sunday morning, a glorious sun rose above the still-vacant site. By 11am the heat was out to greet the earliest arrivals. The first few dozens of vehicles parked right behind the stalls and vans.

As it was really a family occasion, Sunday started out with a picnic. On the stage the sound crew was checking everything out thoroughly. Over a dozen artists were scheduled to perform later, some major names on the international music scene; everything had to be perfect. Above the stage, a huge white banner with black borders spelt: Rastafari Birthday Festival, each word in its own colour — red, gold and green. On either side, the two radio stations sponsoring the event had set up their own small platform. Shortly after midday the first sound vans started to drive onto the grass. The stewards were on hand to locate spots. It wasn't supposed to be a 'first come, first serve' affair, but eventually that's how it turned out. In any case, every set found somewhere to string up. By 2pm some heavy tunes provided the background for the occasion.

The stage show was scheduled to kick off at 3pm but then that, as always, was only an indication. The crowds were coming in thick by now; some by public transport, some by private vehicles. Bicycles were also popular. Coachloads from the main countryside towns came to swell up the ranks of the Londoners.

D. and his people had arrived around 1.30pm. They parked to the left of the stage, behind the line of stalls and spread out to eat lunch. Sweetie, Pam and Bess had been on site from around 10am, dealing with the last minute arrangements, making sure that they were ready to provide the supplies when called upon. Piper, in his role of co-ordinator, had been up and down since Saturday morning. The security teams were discreet but effective, the stewards helpful and good-humoured.

Looking through the crowd from the vantage point of his car boot on which he was sitting, D. was feeling good. He was happy that it had all turned out as he had hoped. The weather especially was perfect. The white silk suit Bess had designed and cut for him, with bands in rasta colours at the sleeves and sides, suited him perfectly. Charlie was beside him sipping a juice, looking equally neat in a shorts and shirt grey and green

111

suit. Their wives and children, after eating, had taken a walk around the stalls. Pablo had disappeared earlier on in the direction of the stage. But Slinga, faithful to his post, was leaning against the car, building a big spliff. Behind them, a sound was testing, running tunes to allow the engineers to adjust for maximum output. High Noon was there, not too far away. Radical was supposed to be on the other side near the stage. No clash for the two rival sounds today. From time to time, the deejays on the radio stations' platforms by the stage would ask for people to come up. A line of metal barriers in front of the stage barely contained the mass of jostling people. Men, women and children of all shapes and descriptions were there, some with cameras, some with cassette recorders, some with whistles, some with binoculars... The noise level was fantastic. On the stage, stacks of amplifiers had been set up, instruments ready for the bands to play. A set of drums of various sizes were being lined up at the front. Finally the time came for the show to start. The radio deejays had been announcing it for fifteen minutes at least. The sound systems turned down their volume. Several crews were anyway now mingling in the crowd and at the back of the stage where a gathering of stars waited in the wings. Onto the stage and up to the microphone stepped Piper. He looked over the sea of bodies. A minute passed, while everyone waited for the white-robed elderly rastaman to say something. He finally cleared his throat and began:

"Greetings to all of you who have come from near and far to celebrate the Rastafari Birthday Festival. Those who were here yesterday had a nice time, I know," he smiled. "I know you've all come to hear good music, not to hear me make a speech, so I'll be brief. I would just like to say that this festival is more than a rasta celebration. It is a celebration of the unity of black people, of the survival of black people, because we were not expected to live and get together again. But we did. Rasta is not only for rastaman, it isn't about hair." Piper held up one of his long greyish dreadlocks. "Rasta is an inner thing, it means spiritual upliftment and material progress."

Piper stopped and looked down. All around nodded. He continued:

"Many years ago Marcus Garvey said, 'what you do today that is worthwhile will inspire others to act at some future time'. This means we need to set examples for the children that will come after us. Do good and good will follow you. I would like to thank all the artists that have been kind enough to come and entertain you, some from very far. Each one of them is special, as each one of you is special. I have asked all the artists to contribute only conscious and positive lyrics for this festival. These two days prove that the love we have for one another is stronger than the system that sets us against one another. So thank you again for being here. Open your hearts and live up! Jah almighty gives us his blessing."

After a short silence, the entire crowd erupted in applause and cheers. The words of the rastaman had touched each one present and for a short instant, they could feel the electricity of the collective elation. Piper was still at the mike.

"I would like all of us, before the show starts, to have a minute of silence as a tribute to all those who are no longer with us, who would have been here today... Let us pay them respect."

For a whole minute, the crowd of thousands stood up and, each one in their own thoughts, paid tribute to their dearly departed. Then Piper announced:

"The first act today represents the foundation, the beginning, because at the beginning of all music is the drum and the voice.

Please welcome The Rasta Gong."

At the same time half a dozen rastaman took position behind the drums on stage. They wasted no time but started right away to chant and beat the skin, the deep throbbing voice of the large bass drum sending tremors through the captivated audience. Out of the PA system the amplified drumming patterns filled the place like waves crashing down. At the back of the stage, the atmosphere was thick with smoke and movement, a happy mix of singers, MCs and friends all huddled and feeling the one beat.

By D. and Charlie's cars, Marcus, Jesse, Carol's two children, Sweetie's son and a few others were jumping wildly, intoxicated by the general euphoria. Jenny, Charmaine, Sweetie and Carol were all there chatting, rocking, looking around for familiar faces. A little way from the cars, Charlie, D., Slinga and a few other acquaintances were sharing smokes and drinks, happy to partake in the heat of the event. It wasn't so often such occasions occurred, when they felt relaxed outdoors and could enjoy themselves without restraint. The crowd of smoke that drifted over Clapham Common testified to the laid-back state of things.

Puggy appeared, two girls in tow and greeted the little group.

"Yo, superstar, what time you due on?" Charlie asked him.

"Around five," Puggy said.

"Alright, you seen Fly?"

Puggy shrugged.

"No. Him seh him would meet me up yah."

Charlie nodded.

"Don't forget, business before pleasure..."

A few more rude boys came through and stopped to talk. Charlie took out a crate of drinks from his boot and the crew got busy on them. All around, people were similarly occupied. Everything was at its best. On the stage, artist after artist came on and gave their all. Some of the acts were major celebrities who just happened to be in the UK, some were residents; all received huge welcomes, performed their best known hits then left the stage reluctantly because there were so many more coming on after them. The sound systems were kicking also. Large crowds had gathered by now around each set, some faithful followers, others just tuning in for the day. The best move was to hop from set to set across the park, staying only a while to take in each one. Clapham Common was 'hot' in all senses of the term.

"Don man, wha' yuh ah seh?"

D. turned and saw Bess in her red shorts and vest with a matching bandana around her head. By now he was on his third stout, just about to pass an acquaintance a good spliff.

"Wait, whe' yuh ah come from?" he asked, dropping some herb into his friend's open palm.

"I don't stop from dis mornin', yuh know."

Bess explained how she'd been busy making sure the food and drinks for the artists were programmed right. She'd left Pam out there to come and find them.

"Me spot your car from de stage, it look wicked, man."

D. smiled.

"Yuh want a spliff?" he asked.

Bess declined.

"Nah man, Piper give me one earlier on, I still feel it..." She added, "I passed by the hospital this morning, still same way..."

D. nodded thoughtfully and took a draw.

"About dis gal," Bess went on, "I want yuh let me deal wid de matter..."

Sweetie had explained to D. how they had found a route to

115

Glenda. D. had welcomed the news but said nothing more. He looked at Bess.

"She an' de bwoy gettin' de same deal, don't worry about dat, man."

But Bess had a fixed idea.

"Listen D., you deal wid de bwoy, but leave de gal to me. Ah my play dat."

D. thought about it. Bess sounded determined.

"Like how yuh jus' fly in', I don't really want yuh fe get ina trouble, yuh understan'?" he said. "She nah get 'way, trust me."

"Yuh cyan do everyt'ing, D. Me know seh too much heat deh 'pon yuh a'ready. Mek me handle dat."

It was hard to say no, Bess was making sense.

"A'right," D. said finally, "but check me first ina de week, seen?"

Bess said she would. She went to check Sweetie and the rest of the women. Shortly after, Jenny arrived with Jesse.

"Your son's looking for you."

D. looked down at his boy and smiled.

"Yuh ah give trouble again?" he asked.

Jesse shook his head with a mischievous grin.

"You alright?" Jenny asked.

"Yeah man, how it go over deh?"

"We're gonna take a walk round the other side. You want him?"

"Yuh can leave him wid me, him safe."

Jesse watched his mother walk off. He was getting taller, but remained slim.

"Yuh want a drink?" D. asked him.

The little boy shook his head.

"Yuh hungry? No... What yuh want?"

Jesse smiled.

"Ice cream," he said, looking straight at his father.

D. laughed.

"Me shoulda know."

Ice cream was Jesse's thing. He simply loved it but his mother only allowed him to have any once in a while. D. stretched and told Charlie that he was going for a walk. Father and son made their way through the groups of people alongside the busy food and drinks stalls and vans. Business was brisk everywhere. D. stopped in front of an ice cream van, but Jesse didn't want those ones. He told D., in his own words, he wanted the tall ones. D. gathered that he meant the soft Italian ice creams, so they walked on. It took ten minutes but they finally found what Jesse wanted. They lined up behind a few other ice cream buyers. Jesse was transfixed, watching the short white man with his apron pull down the lever that released the flow of cream out of the spout. Their turn came, D. ordered a double one for his son. Personally, he wasn't into ice-cream that much. He was paying the man when he heard a familiar voice behind him.

I'll have a double one too!"

D. turned around and found himself looking into Sherry's smiling face.

"Yuh find me!"

Sherry was with Maxine and another friend who stood back a little. Both smiled warmly at D. Sherry said they'd come early and had walked around to see everything.

"The sounds are kicking." she told D.

"Which part Radical set up?"

Sherry pointed to an area by the right side of the stage. She looked down at Jesse, absorbed in his big ice cream.

"You two look alike! How old is he?"

"Almost two," D. said.

Sherry asked Jesse for some ice cream, but his eyes told her 'no'. She looked at D. with a little grin.

"You gonna give me one like him?"

D. squinted at her.

"Behave yourself..."

"Where is his mother ?" Sherry asked

"Somewhere around." D. called out to Maxine. "Thomas lookin' fe yuh."

Maxine pushed out her mouth.

"He's not gonna find me... Not today!"

D. laughed.

"Which part ouno goin' now?" he asked Sherry.

"Further down. High Noon is supposed to be over there."

"Alright, me see yuh later."

"I'll be by Radical later," Sherry said.

"I meet yuh down there."

Sherry and her two friends left. Jesse's ice cream had started melting. D. tried to show him how to cope with it. A sudden huge roar saluted the arrival on stage of the most popular Jamaican artist of the moment. He'd been touring the UK and Europe and his appearance at this festival sent his numerous fans into a frenzy. D. lifted Jesse onto his shoulders high above the crowd. Instead of tracking back the way they came, D. decided to take another route, behind the stalls. People were standing up on car roofs everywhere to get a better view of the stage. One attractive girl with a drink in her hand pointed D. and his son out to her friend, smiling.

"Hi," she said as they passed her.

D. smiled back and said "Hi," but didn't stop. They continued alongside a mass of people gathered around one of the sets. The rhythms were heavy, pumping raw energy through the dancers. A little further, a group of white people, probably tourists, were gesticulating with careless abandon to the sounds of another set. Jesse was still licking his ice cream. As they passed by a cluster of cars, D. heard a shout:

"Yush...! Yush...!"

He scanned the surroundings. He knew the call was for him. His gaze turned towards a white Mercedes a few yards away. Two youths were standing in front of it, stepping to the music floating across from a nearby set. Behind them, D. could make out the face of someone staring in his direction. The man, dark glasses obscuring his features, stood up from behind the open door of the car. D. recognised who it was; he hesitated for a few seconds, cautiously observing the people around the car, ready for anything. But this was holiday... Anyway, the man was smiling. D. put Jesse down and walked him towards the Mercedes. The man slammed the driver's door shut and stood by the car looking at D. and his son approaching, a plastic cup in his right hand. He was dressed neatly, his shirt open, a thick gold chain over his vest. The two youths in front of the car threw D. a casual glance and continued dancing. D. stopped, holding Jesse by the hand.

"Missa D., long time... Wha' yuh ah seh?" Joseph asked.

D. nodded.

"Cool yuh know. Wha' ah gwan?"

Joseph seemed in a good mood.

"I jus' coolin' off." He smiled at Jesse. "Hi junior, gimme some ice cream nuh?"

That was unlikely. Jesse looked at him then simply ignored him.

"Relax man," Joseph told D. "Me jus' see yuh pass an' call yuh. Mek me an' yuh talk..."

D. was still wary of the man.

"Talk 'bout wha'?" he asked coldly.

119

Joseph laughed and took a sip from his cup.

"D. man, me an' yuh nuh have no problem, y'know."

They didn't, D. knew that.

"True," he said. Then he asked, "How is t'ings?"

Joseph shrugged.

"So-so y'know. Me did wan' see yuh 'bout somet'ing."

D. let go of Jesse's hand. The little boy was watching two youngsters kicking a football nearby. Joseph could sense D.'s uneasiness. He sighed.

"Look man, I want yuh fe know seh me nah carry no feelings, seen? What happen before done settle, so everyt'ing level."

It sounded like a genuine peace talk. Their last encounter had been unfriendly, but then D was vexed at the time...

"Me an' yuh nah have no quarrel, Joseph," he said.

Joseph smiled behind his glasses, held up his cup,

"Yuh want a drink ?"

"Wha' dat?"

"Rum, man."

D. grinned

"I cyan really handle it right now."

Joseph laughed.

"Have a beer, man." He called out to the youth at the front. "Yaow, Sly, get a beer for de man!"

The tallest of the two youths walked to the car boot, opened it and took out a bottle of Red Stripe. He opened the top and handed it to D. Jesse was finishing his ice cream. Joseph emptied his cup. He turned to D.

"Yuh see Lancey?"

The question was direct. D. wasn't really surprised about the topic. He nodded gravely, pouring a little of his beer on the grass.

"Wha' him seh to yuh?" Joseph asked.

D. took a swig and shook his head.

"Him seh him ah de sheriff," he smirked.

"Yuh know wha' him come for?" Joseph asked.

D. paused, then said: "All I know is him don't like me, from time, an' I don't like him neither."

"De man is bad news, me ah tell yuh, D."

Lancey sure was.

"Bad news fe me; him nah trouble ouno," D. said.

Joseph looked at him.

"Enh? Yuh don't know Lancey, man."

He paused to pick up a bottle of rum inside the car, poured himself some and replaced the bottle. D. was thinking. He told Joseph:

"Fe years, Lancey ah try diss me. But is jus' t'rough Skeets did look after me, he couldn't really do it."

Joseph took a sip of his rum and swallowed. He studied D. for a few seconds.

"What Skeets tell yuh 'bout Lancey?" he asked.

"Him seh Lancey ah one vicious police, love kill people," D. replied. "But him seh Lancey wouldn't face him."

Joseph laughed, took off his glasses and put them down on the car roof.

"Yuh know why?"

"Skeets badder dan him," D. stated.

"Ah true," Joseph nodded. " 'Nuff people respect Skeets. But Lancey ah police an' 'if him really wan' dus' somebody, him always find a way. Notin' no devious like him."

Out of his shirt pocket, Joseph took out a packet of cigarettes and offered one. D. declined. Joseph lit up and blew out the smoke.

"Lancey earn 'nuff money t'rough Skeets, yuh know," Joseph explained. "Yuh know seh Lancey used to work fe Skeets?"

D. frowned.

"Work fe him?"

"Yeah man," Joseph confirmed. "Me ah talk long time, before Skeets bring yuh in."

D. shook his head incredulous. Joseph went on.

"Lancey used to do security work fe Skeets for a couple of years. Then him go an' join de police. Is even Skeets sort out certain papers fe him, talk to some people, yuh know what I mean...?"

D. nodded, taking in the story. Joseph pulled hard on his cigarette, digging up memories.

"After Lancey join de force," he continued, "him still did work fe Skeets. Dem time, shipments jus' start fe come t'rough and Skeets was organisin' de business. Dat was when I started..."

"So... Lancey did involve ina de runnings then?" D. asked, trying to figure out the whole picture.

"As a police, Lancey was more useful to Skeets. Anytime somet'ing happen down ah Central him know 'bout it. When Skeets moved some stuff, Lancey mek sure de way clear fe dat. Him jus turn a blind eye, everyt'ing was runnin' smooth."

"Then what happen?" D. asked.

Joseph drank some more rum.

"What happen? One police find out certain t'ings was goin' on, Lancey couldn't buy him... so him dus' him."

"Lancey kill a nex' police?"

D. couldn't believe it.

"Dat bwoy deadly, me ah tell yuh...!" Joseph said somberly. "Him set up de other officer, pay some gunman to ambush him then him kill de gunman himself."

Even though D. was himself no angel and had seen some bad things in his time, the story sounded ugly. He thought about it for a while, then asked:

122

"Him get 'way wid it?"

Joseph shrugged.

"Some police did suspect him, but dem couldn't prove notin', so dem move him out."

D. nodded.

"Yeah, me 'member dat."

"Anyway, from dat time Skeets couldn't use Lancey no more. So him start work fe de politicians dem."

D. knew that part. Lancey had gotten promotion by working his way in with the politicians, providing personal security for the top men. It all made sense. Skeets knew too much about Lancey for him to turn against his ex-employer. Joseph could see D.'s mind was working, shaping up the whole story. He told him:

"One t'ing yuh mus' understan' 'bout Lancey, star: no matter how it go, him haffe get pay. Dat is all him worry 'bout. Anyt'ing ah gwan him mus' get fe him cut."

"Him cyaan touch you though," D. said.

Joseph looked at him.

"Comin like yuh nah understan': him wan' everybody fe pay dues, all ah we."

"Wha', but... Skeets?"

"Him don't see it like dat. Ah me him ah deal wid, not Skeets. An' like how dem send him up yah, ah fe him big chance dat. Him haffe get some pounds!"

D. could see what was happening now. They had sent Lancey over to help the English police but he had his own agenda. It must have been like a dream come true for the Jamaican officer. They had put a fox in charge of a fowl coop...!

Joseph glanced at D., sipped some rum before saying:

"Somet'ing else yuh don't know." He paused. "I don't even know if I should tell yuh dis..."

"Say wha'?" D. asked intrigued.

Joseph was silent for a while. He looked around cautiously. D. noticed Jesse coming back his way.

"Yuh 'member when yuh bus' ina my house, after Blue shot yuh?"

D. remembered, but that was old business. Joseph could see what he was thinking. He smiled.

"Cool man, as I say: me nuh carry no feelings, yuh had to do it. "

Then he continued.

"I realised then why Blue did wan' fe kill yuh. But I couldn't tell yuh, yuh understan'."

D. understood. He sipped some beer.

"Yuh nevah know seh police did arrest Blue fe killin' yuh breddah."

D. glared at Joseph, very still. Joseph stood the stare.

"Yeah man, dem arrest him. Lock him up. But dem let him go after coupla days."

A lot of things were going through D.'s head. Jesse came and held his hand, he looked down at his son. He didn't press Joseph, he knew there was more to come.

"Someone destroyed de papers and de evidene, there was no witnesses. Blue get out an' lef' Jamaica." Joseph looked at D. He knew he was smart enough to work it out.

"Lancey..." D. said simply.

"Lancey." Joseph repeated, nodding.

"Why?" D. asked.

Joseph's rum was finished, he threw the plastic cup on the grass.

"Why? Because by dat time Lancey was runnin' fe him own traffic. Him learn a lot from Skeets an' set up a lickle operation fe himself. Blue was movin' de stuff fe him. Him had to spring him outta jail."

D. took it in, then asked one more question.

"Skeets did know?"

"Skeets always know everyt'ing. Lancey was double-crossing him, but him jus' hol' it down. Him couldn't tell you either. Yuh woulda get yuhself killed. An' Skeets didn't want dat."

Everything made sense now. Skeets had brought D. up and kept him out of reach of Lancey who had one more reason to want him dead. If D. had known he would have tried to avenge his brother, but at the time he wasn't ready. Skeets knew that. Joseph looked at D.

"Yuh know de whole story now," he said. "But remember; yuh don't get it from me, seen?"

D. nodded. In a way he was grateful to Joseph. But he had a bitter taste in his mouth. Joseph sighed.

"Dat is de way dis business run, D. Yuh cyaan trust no one. Nobody's clean."

The words played on D.'s mind for a little while. The sun was still hot above, music was still filling the air and the crowds were all happy and dancing, but D. wasn't really feeling like that no more. His mind had travelled to 'back then'. Jesse tugged at his hand, calling him back.

"Lancey try tax yuh yet?" Joseph asked.

"Me buck him up at de hospital whe' day, when my soldier get shot."

"Mmmn, me hear 'bout dat," Joseph said. "So what happen?"

"Right now, me out fe deal wid dat," D. assured him.

He paused and put down his empty bottle.

"Yuh ah hear me, Joseph? Comin' like Lancey number call."

Joseph looked at him.

"Watch out fe him, man. Ah one vicious bwoy. Original dog heart."

D. didn't answer. He had a lot of thinking to do.

"I gwan mek a move, seen? So, more time," he said.

"Yes man, if anyt'ing, yuh know whe' me deh."

Before walking away, D. stretched out his right fist. Joseph touched him.

"Ah de vibes man;" he said, "today ah rasta festival..."

"True."

D. left with Jesse. They continued alonsgide the stalls until they were back by the cars where their little group strained to see Puggy and Firefly who had just walked on stage.

The two artists got into their act right away, sending all the young, and less young, women in the front row wild. Their voices came out clear through the PA's speaker stacks. Puggy was up and down, jumping and crossing the length of the stage, working the crowd. Firefly's lyrics were flawless as usual, his voice getting stronger with each verse. Their set lasted only about fifteen minutes, short and sweet as thy say. They managed to do one encore, their current release which was fast climbing the charts. Charlie looked quite satisfied with his artists' performance. D.'s mind was still pondering the conversation with Joseph, he couldn't help that. Jenny had noticed his face when he handed Jesse back to her. She knew him enough to notice things like that. But D. told her he was okay. She didn't persist.

"Don, Piper did ask fe yuh," Slinga informed his boss.

There were still a few acts to go on stage, though the afternoon was drawing towards evening. In an hour or so, the sun would go down. The sounds would probably play until as late as possible, though the police were sure to try and close them down early.

D. called to Charlie.

"I want to go an' check backstage."

Charlie also felt like doing that. Accompanied by Slinga, they made their way together through the crowd. Backstage, they found Puggy surrounded by a crowd of admirers, Firefly close by with a smaller group of friends. Most of the artists who had already performed were there, except those who had gone to sing and deejay on the various sound systems. Charlie congratulated the pair, D. too.

"I wan' go chat 'pon Radical," Puggy said. He seemed full of energy, hungry for a microphone.

"The vibes ketch yuh, man," D. told him.

"Pure new lyrics me 'ave today."

Puggy motioned towards Firefly.

"My yout' yah ah get wicked, yah know Charlie."

Finally, they all made their way to Radical who'd set up a hundred yards away. Puggy pushed through to the control tower, where Max was running things hot. Everywhere you looked, masses of people rocked and jumped to his selection. The area around the set was smoky, vibrant with shouts and noises of all kinds. Girls of all shapes and styles were there in abundance, some doing the Bogle, some the Armstrong, some the Limbo, and various other dances of the moment. Max had just got the crowd screaming with a new Shabba single. The Grammy MC was riding a rhythm with consummate skill, and in line with the day's accent on conscious lyrics, was urging all new artists to respect the elder entertainers. The needle lifted up.

"Shabba!" Max shouted into the mike. Then he greeted Puggy who had just made it to the controls. "Massive, too much artists in the area. Lickle more, live an' direck, Puggy, the loverman, fe real. Now hear dis...!" Shabba came back again and kicked it heavy.

Before he changed the record, Max sent some dedications to

the crew to his right:

"Big up D., Charlie and the crew. Firefly, your bredrin jus' tell me yuh deh yah. Step up, man!"

A touch of sound effects and another rhythm punched its way through the big speakers framing the area. Max was on the case, sending some hard styles to his audience's heads and they in return were urging him on to even greater heights. Most of the big names got a touch on the turntable, though Max kept out any slack or gun lyrics, as all sets had been asked to do for the day. Terror Fabulous, Jigsy King, Capleton, Mega Banton, and Jigsy King again together with Barrngton Levy, on a wicked tune urging all posses to 'work', all got played before Puggy finally took the mike. By that time the crowd was well excited. Puggy opened up by sending his dedications.

"All girls, brownings and ebonies, big up ouno status."

Then he sent a few requests out to D, Charlie his manager, and a few other people before getting down to work. Then Firefly found his way up and the two did a two-in-one combination to the delight of the audience. D. and Charlie were doing their thing amidst the dancers. Slinga had followed Puggy to the set. Max touched down on some Cutty Ranks, Tony Rebel and Lieutenant Stitchie to follow *Deportee* by Buju Banton. By the set, Slinga's hand rose high above his head in a gun salute, while he showed off the latest 'gangsta' dance style from Jamaica.

The next tune started at slow speed, on purpose — Buju's voice distorted — then it stopped. But those few seconds had been enough to raise the already vulcanic temperature in the crowd. The deafening clamour, punctuated by simulated gunshots of various calibres, forced the selector to pull up one of Buju Banton's most famous tunes. Max laughed purposefully into the live microphone.

"Alright... yuh see dis? Hol' on...!"

He could hardly get himself heard above the tumult.

"Radical massive, hear dis: yuh see today, ah strickly rasta business, seen?!"

The shouts continued.

"Dat means... me haffe play dis."

Puggy took up the mike and stirred it up further.

"Fe real, rude yout'! Dis is a *yatty*man-free area."

Max let the record go. Once again the noise level went up a few decibels. It was the right time to drop it. The way the crowd felt by now, Max couldn't have selected a better tune. The controversy surrounding Buju's record had made the young ghetto MC a kind of unofficial ambassador for reggae music, especially amongst the hardcore ragga youth. Max lifted up the needle once more. He shouted:

"Respeck to all raggamuffins. *Boom Bye Bye* continually, seen?!"

With that the music started again, accompanied by a choir of voices from the audience. D. was in the mood too, not to mention Charlie whose favourtie record it was. Back to back, Max flung down the no-less virulent Red Dragon record on the same topic to the continued approval of his audience.

D. remembered he was supposed to check Piper. Caught in the Radical vibe, it had almost slipped his mind. He told Charlie before walking off. He stepped away from the dancing crowd and headed for the stage. Behind him, he heard Max shouting through the loudspeakers:

"Without any apologies, rude bwoy!"

On the performance stage, the penultimate artist was performing. There were now even more people backstage. D. asked a woman he knew for Piper's whereabouts. She pointed to the far corner. When he got there, he found the dread with another rasta brethren, sitting between the stage and the large equipment van. Piper's brethren was attaching a long, plastic tube to the small end of the cow horn in his hand. It had been a while since D. had seen that type of chalice. Piper looked up from the board where he was busy cutting a portion of herb.

"Come in, me lion. Me did ah look fe yuh."

D. leaned against the van, watching the two dreads prepare the chalice. Both sides of the narrow passage, groups of people were burning herb and talking. The festival was a great success. Everyone felt high, no one seemed ready to go home.

The sun was huge on the horizon, sinking slowly. Piper had finished cutting the herb fine, he dipped his fingers in a cup of water next to him and sprinkled the board a few times. Then he proceeded to load the kutchie — the clay cone used for burning — careful not to fill it too tight. The brethren passed him the water-filled horn and Piper affixed the kutchie onto it. Everything was ready. Piper looked satisfied.

"Yes I, de pipe ready fe burn." He asked his bredrin, "Zebbie, de I know dat yout' deh?"

Zebbie scrutinised D., trying to recognise his face.

"Ah Jerry lickle breddah, yuh know," Piper said.

The dread looked again, a faint smile on his lips. He stroked his bushy beard thoughtfully and nodded.

"True, true. Love I."

"Irie bredrin," D. replied.

"Lion, de man wan' share de cup wid' I an' I?" Piper asked.

D. hadn't touched a chalice for years, many years, yet he could not really refuse.

"Yes rasta, nice..."

He squatted down between the two dreads. Piper pulled some matches out of his trouser pocket and placed them on the ground before him. He handed the chalice to Zebbie.

130

"De man fe light it, Iya."

The rastaman took the pipe ceremoniously; it was a mark of respect. Piper then formed his two hands into an open triangle, in the traditional manner and started the blessing.

"Glory be to Jah almighty, the maker of Creation. His blessing be upon us as we share dis herb. As it was in de beginnin', is now an' ever shall be, world without end. Jah Rastafari."

D. was surprised to find he remembered the prayer. A long buried memory...

Then Piper picked up the matches, took out three sticks and lit them. Zebbie blew some air through his nostrils and started to pull on the tube as the fire embraced the green herb in the kutchie. Zebbie drew long and hard, the top of the kutchie was red hot. Out of the horn, you could hear the soft bubbling of the water. The cloud of smoke that flowed out of Zebbie's nostrils engulfed the three men, thick and white. Piper tapped the mouth of the kutchie while Zebbie pulled again. After another cloud, he uttered a blessing and passed the chalice to Piper.

Squatting amidst the smoke, the pungent smell already playing on his senses, D. watched Piper draw on the chalice, 'cooking' it slowly until he'd built up the heat. Then, with one last deep pull, he kicked it alight. Only a bonafide rastaman knew how to burn a chalice in this way. The intake of herb would drop any uninitiated smoker...

Once he was done, Piper passed the chalice on to D. The kutchie was deep, there was still a good amount of herb inside. D. blew out some air; cleared his mind of bad thoughts. Today seemed to be a day for flashbacks. He recalled his early days now, when he'd started out in the rastaman way, in Jerry's back yard...

D. brought the tube to his lips, his left hand held the horn.

131

One finger over the hole in the horn to block the air, he started to pull, gradually. The water bubbled but he needed a deeper pull. He started again. This time the herb in the kutchie was burning, he could hear it. D. stoked the fire sharply and pulled hard, taking in a lungfull of herb. He held it in before blowing out. He saw Piper's eyes narrow, through the drifting white smoke. D. coughed a little; the herb was clearing his throat. His second pull on the chalice was sharper now he'd gotten back the hang of it. He kicked it hot. When he had finished he found he was light, clear, feeling close to the two dreadlocks without even speaking to them. Zebbie cleaned up the kutchie. Piper looked at D.

"Jah herb, de healin' of de nation, de spirutal upliftment of de people," he said in a low voice.

"Sensimilla," D. answered. His mind was tuned to the meaning of Piper's words. Many times as a youth he had sat and listened as Jerry and his brethren smoked and reasoned for hours. He pulled up a crate nearby and sat. Zebbie studied him briefly, then turned to Piper.

"Today is a blessed day. I an' I love to see black people gather ina one inity."

Piper smiled.

"All turn out well, positive vibes, togetherness," he added. "Music is de key, is music bring de nation together."

"De right music," Zebbie said.

"Yes, Iya, de right music — positive reggae music. Yuh see when cultural music ah play, nobody nah fight. Music influence everyt'ing."

"Reggae music international!" D. heard himself saying.

"Ah dat promote Jamaica."

Zebbie agreed.

"Yes, me breddah. Jamaica bring out de message to de world.

132

Dat is why we haffe keep playin' de right music, yuh nuh see't."

"Me lion, yuh see Jamaica...?" Piper started. "Jamaica 'ave 'nuff potential, yuh know. Right now 'nuff black people don't realise how important Jamaica is."

D. agreed.

"Jamaica lead the way, rasta. Out of Jamaica, Marcus Garvey speak out fe all black people."

"Marcus!" Zebbie exclaimed with a dreamy smile.

Piper nodded.

"Marcus Garvey, de prophet. All up to now, years after, none ah dem politician an' so-call leader even achieve wha' Marcus do."

"False shepherds," Zebbie said.

"Jah himself inspire Marcus to go all over de world' to gather black people."

D. coughed then said:

"The man get so powerful, it tek de whole U.S. government fe stop him. One lickle black man..."

"America, de belly ah de beast," Zebbie nodded.

"When yuh check it out, dem people frighten fe see black man get strong," Piper reflected.

"Prophecy mus' fulfil," Zebbie said forcefully.

For a while, the reasoning circled around the scriptures, Piper expounding on the Book of Revelations, Zebbie an' D. confirming his points.

Zebbie said with a knowing smile, "Ah dat mek Reagan an' him bwoy dem burn down de herb ah Yard, dem 'fraid seh I an' I get wise."

"Jah herb bring we together, rasta. When man an' man smoke, dem will talk an' reason. Nobody want to quarrel an' fight."

"True, dread. Herb mek a man meditate, look ina himself."

"Dat is wha' de Bible seh, know yuhself... "

The reasoning could have carried on till dawn, but with darkness gradually setting down on the park, the festival was folding up. A little while later, D. took his leave of the two brethren, feeling peaceful, his mind cool and calm. Now that the stage show had ended, everyone had retreated to the sounds which were still rocking the crowd. D. didn't feel like returning to Radical. Leisurely, he made his way down to find his family.

D. drove Jenny and Jesse home. He ate and sat in front of the TV but wasn't really watching it. Jenny went to bed. D. switched off the TV and sat there for a while. Then he got up and left the house, drove to the Spot and spent some time there making sure all was well. But he didn't feel like staying; the chalice had put him in a meditative mood and he found that the atmosphere in the club didn't suit him tonight. He split around 1.30am and swung the car in the direction of Donna's place.

Once inside, he opened the living room windows to let some air in. He picked up the phone and stretched across the couch, shoes off. When he dialled, no one answered at first. In Jamaica it was still late afternoon. After a few more rings, there was a voice at the other end.

"Hello, who's speaking, please?"
"Cindy, what happen?"
"Hi D., you alright?"
Cindy proceeded to fill D. in on her activities of the past few days.

He had to interrupt her in mid-flight to ask for her mother. Donna came on.

"D., wha' yuh ah seh? Yuh suppose to call Wednesday."

"Yeah true... but I was busy. So how ouno stay?"

"We alright. We jus' come back from country."

Donna had gotten Leroy to drive them to St. Ann's to visit his cousin Thomas and his family as D. had asked her to. She said they were all well. She and the children had spent three days there before Leroy returned for them.

"Dem love Avril, yuh see man!"

Donna informed D. of how his daughter had been feted by everyone in the village and how she had to resist requests by Cassie, Thomas' wife, to keep Avril. She added, laughing:

"She bust her mout' down deh."

"Wha, Wha'ppen?"

"She alright, man," Donna reassured D.

"Then, how yuh ah laugh, Donna man?"

"She alright, she jus' cut her lip that's all. Stop fretting."

Once D. was reassured about his daughter he asked about the business Donna had been looking after. She said all was settled, then added:

"Leroy gwan stay over, so him can start de work fe yuh."

"So when yuh comin' back?" D. asked.

"Next week Sunday. Yuh tek care ah de rent an' de bills, like how me ask yuh?"

"Everyt'ing alright man, don't worry. So how t'ings stay?"

"Bwoy it rough a way over yah, yuh know. Oh yes, de barrel dem reach, Friday. Me an' Leroy go an' clear dem out. My auntie said 'T'ank yuh.'"

"Yuh gi' 'way de rest ah de t'ings dem."

"Yeah man, your bredrin dem well happy. Yuh wan' see everybody ah model de clothes an' shoes yuh send dem. Dem tell me fe t'ank *yuh, dem ah big yuh up everywhere."*

D. smiled to himself. He knew his old friends in the area would appreciate the gesture.

"Yuh get your car?" Donna asked.

"Yeah man, it wicked. Sammy set it up nice."

"So yuh ah drive up an' down wid your gal now?"

D. kissed his teeth.

"Is wha' happen to yuh? Yuh ask me fe call yuh so yuh can cuss me?"

"Is alright. Me ah come back soon, t'ings gwan change."

"Jus' cool, Donna man... So wha' yuh have money left?"

"Not much, I give some to Cassie, also to Maas Zack daughter like you told me. Yuh can send some fe Leroy to start de work, I don't need much now."

"Alright, me send a money Wednesday. Whe' Avril deh?"

"She's sleepin'. Dat gal always up an' down all day... So how Charlie dem?"

"Everybody alright."

Donna and D. talked some more. It was easy to forget the distance, Donna sounded so close. D. didn't worry too much about the bill. He missed his woman and daughter, even Cindy. Donna and he had not been on very good terms before she left but that was forgotten now. He would be glad to see her, he told her so.

"So yuh miss me now, so yuh say."

"Yuh don't believe me?"

"Then how yuh treat me so bad when me deh 'bout?"

"Don't seh dat man, jus' sometimes... De pressure, y'know?"

"Yes, I know," Donna said. *"Yuh bettah sort out yuhself an' come home. Even Thomas ask me fe tell yuh him have some land him lookin' after fe yuh. Him seh fe come an' work wid him when yuh ready."*

D. said he was thinking about it. After a little while, and some more

136

man/woman 'fencing', Donna told D. he should get some rest. She always worried about his welfare. D. said he'd call back in the week, before sending the money.

D. didn't move for some time after replacing the receiver. His mind drifted back through his old neighbourhood, over the fences and down the alleys, all the way to his village in the hills, through the cultivated fields and the steep gullies.

For over a year it had become almost a ritual. Every other Saturday, same time same place. The shoppers were milling around the car park, wheeling trolleys, loading car boots with full carrier bags. Sitting in the passenger seat of his car, Simon wished he was miles away, some place else in better company. Amongst all the unpleasant things he had to get through to get to his goal this had to be the one he hated the most. Beside him, the man was lighting another cigarette, smoke drifted out of the open window. Simon couldn't quite pinpoint what he disliked the most about him; the protruding stomach, the smell of his cheap aftershave or the saggy bags under his green eyes. In fact he hated every bone in the man's body. He had no choice but to bear him until he could finally move away from this ugly scene. He felt nothing but scorn for what the man was and the fat, balding Inspector in turn treated him with contempt. A sound basis for a durable 'partnership'...

"Look, this can't go on any longer. I can't afford it, alright?"

The white man smirked.

"You seem prosperous enough." He glanced at Simon's Jaguar parked in the next space.

"I'm telling you I want this fucker out of my life. You supposed to look after me, that's what I'm paying all this money for, ain'it?"

The policeman looked straight at him.

"Don't get cocky with me, son. You're a big shot, that's why you attract attention."

"Yeah, mainly greedy cops..." Simon sneered.

The man shrugged, blew out some smoke.

"It's all in the game. My problem with your friend is that he's trying to take over what's not his."

"So what you gonna do about it?"

"I need a little time, this is a sensitive situation."

"Time? In my case time is money. Now you know, I'm not paying him a penny more."

The man laughed, not very heartily.

"Yeah, well... watch yourself. I've heard that he's kinda heavy-handed."

Simon frowned. He was holding back the insults that he would have loved to fling in the cop's face.

"Alright calm down, I'll see what can be done. He's not exactly 'flavour of the month' at the nick, you know what I mean? He's bound to slip up soon."

The man paused, threw out the cigarette butt. He sighed heavily.

"We can't have that nigger working my patch can we?"

He caught Simon's gaze.

"What's the matter, don't take it like that. I mean you're more like us really, ain't you. He's a bloody foreigner."

Simon didn't like the 'nigger' in question but couldn't quite see the fine distinction the policeman was making. He had no illusion about the Detective Inspector, racism was part of the job.

"Look, I've got to go," Simon said finally.

"Listen, don't get upset. I'm working on it. We just have to give him a little push, that's all. If he gets caught red-handed, they'll send him back. The sooner the better."

Simon opened the door of the car and mumbled.

"Yeah, meanwhile he's getting fat on me."

The policeman switched on the engine. He smiled, a cold yellow-toothed smile.

"Don't take it so hard, sunshine. Look at it as a temporary tax rise. See you later."

Simon got out and slammed the door shut. He watched the car drive out of parking towards the exit.

'That bastard's got a fat envelope in his pocket, he can afford to be relaxed', he thought to his disgust as he climbed into his car. Days like these, Simon felt like leaving the whole thing and doing what he really wanted to do. But he knew this was the only game in town which could get him the funds he needed in the shortest period of time. Another five, six months at the most he kept telling himself, and he was out of it. That alone kept him going. The days couldn't come quick enough. Feeling gloomy, he turned onto the main road and headed for Stamford Hill. Everything had seemed so promising at first, he had it all planned. Now he was too deep into it and whether he admitted it to himself or not, he was caught in a roller coaster he had no control over. His enemies wanted his blood. The police sponged off all his earnings and Butch was in hospital with a broken spine. Suddenly Simon was feeling very alone, a stranger in his own town. He needed to get away, somewhere where he could take time out from this quagmire and think clearly. Hopefully, the week after next he'd be in Spain. He swung the big car to the right by the library. Right now he didn't want to talk to anyone, except Julie maybe. He'd go to

Satellite later, but for now he needed some rest to get his mind back on course.

Bells, there were bells ringing but he couldn't tell where from. And they didn't sound like bells exactly, but more like gongs... deep sounding; with an echo that made the floor shake under his feet. He wanted to lift himself up from his seat and get to the front where he could see the bridgeroom's face. The bride was veiled and kept turning to look at the guests. The groom simply stood motionless. He stood up stiffly. Then his body started rocking. Why? What was happening now...? Someone was calling, he tried to hang on, he needed to stay there and find out... But the voice called again.

"D...! D...!"

His eyes opened, it took him a few seconds to recognise the face looking down at him.

"Are you alright?"

D. mopped his brow and breathed in deeply. Jenny was staring at him, a concerned look on her face.

"Yeah..." D. mumbled, realising where he was.

Jenny felt his forehead.

"You're sweating."

D. sat up and looked around the bedroom. It was dark, apart from the screen of the portable TV in the corner. He got up from the bed, still unsteady on his feet and went to the bathroom. The cold water felt nice, soothing like a caress on his skin. D. dried up his face and head and sat on the edge of the bath focusing his thoughts. The dreams again...

Each time it was like a trip, a journey from which he didn't

140

want to return. D. couldn't remember all of this one but he knew it had a meaning, there always was. People back home always said dreaming of a wedding was bad news. In general it meant a funeral. D. blew some air through his lips. His throat felt dry but he was calmer now. He left the bathroom and picked up a bottle of water in the kitchen fridge. Back in the bedroom, Jenny was sitting in bed watching a movie.

"You told me to wake you up at one, but I thought something was wrong with you. The way you were tossing and turning... You okay?"

"Yeah man, I'm alright," D. said.

He sat on the corner of the bed and drank some more water. Jenny had gotten used to the dreams that stirred D. in his sleep once every so often. D. had explained that that was the way he was; since childhood dreams had always played an important part in his life.

"What was it about?" Jenny asked.

D. shook his head.

"A wedding," he said.

Jenny smiled.

"You're already married."

"Fe real."

Jenny didn't know the significance of dreams, there was no point in getting her worried. A digital dial on the radio read 12.27. D. got up and walked to the half-opened window. The night was cool and quiet outside. He left Jenny and returned to the bathroom to shower and get ready. Then he chose some clothes, carefully as always. Once dressed, he had a last check in the mirror.

"Jesse alright?" D. asked Jenny, as he picked up his watch and ring from the dresser.

"He was waiting for you to wake up, I told him not to disturb you."

Before leaving, D. playfully provoked Jenny a little, poked her in the ribs, squeezed the back of her neck, all the things he knew she disliked.

"I soon come," he said picking up his phone.

"T'm not waiting up ," she answered.

She knew he was unlikely to be back before daylight.

On his way out D. went to check on his son. The little boy was asleep on his back, as usual, snoring a little, the sheet pushed away. D. tenderly touched the hand which hung over the edge of the bed and left.

Downstairs everything was quiet. In this part of town there wasn't much activity on Saturday nights, not many parties either. D. climbed in his car, selected a cassette and drove out. Before heading for the Spot, he decided to pass by the house in Leyton.

Slinga and Puggy were drinking beer while watching a video of a stage show. The two youths greeted D. Puggy got him a beer. D. sat and watched the show with them. Super Cat, the Apache, was on stage, wilding up a sizeable crowd to fever pitch.

"Which part dat show deh?" D. asked

"Miami," Slinga answered.

Supercat was his favourite artist, he'd gotten the video from his brother in the States and had it converted. Puggy was enjoying every minute of it.

"Wicked lyrics!" he exclaimed as the Apache began 'chatting' over a tune.

D. agreed.

"Yeah man, Cat dangerous..."

"Sherry phone fe yuh," Puggy informed D.

D. should have called her since Tuesday, but he had had a lot on his mind. He sipped some beer and built himself a spliff to relax. Around 2pm, he decided it was time to go. Slinga and Puggy got up also and all three men left together. In the car, D. turned to Puggy:

"Wait, I t'ink seh yuh suppose to check yuh fat gal tonight." He turned to Slinga. "Not dat him seh earlier on?"

"Run him ah run from de work," Slinga said.

D. laughed. Puggy defended himself.

"Nah man, dat gal yah see too much ah me. I don't want her fe tek set."

Puggy had such a busy schedule he had learned to pace himself.

As they drove through Clapton, they noticed a crowd gathered around an ambulance and a couple of police cars in front of a club. Saturday was a bad night for driving on these streets. Cars were cutting, crossing and overtaking anyhow and anywhere. D. sped to Finsbury Park and turned left at the lights, left again then eased off the BMW around a back street corner. The three got out and walked slowly towards the club. There seemed to be quite a few people inside already. A couple of mini cabs were dropping off their fares. Three girls were coming up from the club, talking excitedly amongst themselves. Puggy stopped them.

"Wha'ppen, ouno leavin' a'ready?"

"We're going to a party," one of the girls told him.

The singer didn't want to let them go that easy. D. and Slinga continued down towards the basement entrance. A few ravers were paying dues at the entrance. Costa saw his boss coming and stepped up to clear the way for him.

"Wha'ppen, supa?"

Costa wasn't usually very talkative. Yet tonight he had something to say.

"Lancey deh yah. Him reach 'bout hour ago."

D. frowned and paused before asking:

"Him one?"

Costa nodded.

"Him ask fe yuh. I buy him one drink on de house. Him been drinkin' since dat."

D. had been expecting Lancey to find him for some time now. He knew very well that the officer would hear about the Spot sooner or later. He was about to turn to go down the stairs when Costa added:

"Him don't let me search him..."

D. nodded and told Costa:

"Send ah yout' outside to keep watch."

Then he went down, Slinga following.

Downstairs the place was quite full despite the relatively early hour. The set was kicking, and numerous women were moving appreciatively on the dance floor. In the club's first room, D. answered a few greetings and walked on to the bar. The brown youth behind interrupted what he was doing when he saw D. and motioned towards the left corner, where Lancey was sitting, his back to D. and talking in a girl's ear. Several drinks were lined up on the counter in front of him. The barman lifted the trap to allow D. and Slinga through to the back room. D. expected the call when it came:

"Yaow! Don man, wha' ah gwan?"

He turned and looked towards Lancey. The man had been drinking, you could tell by his eyes.

"Cool, me jus' come," D. answered not very warmly.

Lancey eased off his stool. He was wearing one of those suits he seemed so fond of, light blue with red shirt and black tie. D. signalled to the barman to let him through then opened up the door to the back room. He stepped in. Pablo was sitting behind the desk, watching TV. He got up and greeted D.

"We have a visitor," D. told him, then went to sit in the armchair. Slinga positioned himself by the door, Pablo against the back wall, behind D. Lancey stepped in, a falsely jovial smile on his face.

"So wha'ppen, D.? I been lookin' fe yuh?"

He picked up a chair and sat in front of the desk, uninvited. Slinga closed the door shut behind him.

"It look like yuh find me," D. said.

The TV sound was no more than a buzz, drowned by the bass booming next door. Lancey sat back in the chair. He unbuttoned his jacket and scratched his close-cropped hair.

"Is a nice place yuh 'ave, man."

"A small operation," D. said modestly.

"Nice man, nice," Lancey repeated appreciatively.

D. knew well what the man was getting at, but he played it cool. Slinga and Pablo were standing motionless, apparently watching the TV but their eyes never really strayed from Lancey.

"Is only dis week I find out where yuh ah hide," Lancey grinned.

"Hide? I nevah hide," D. answered, "but me busy more time..."

"Me know," Lancey said, "so how is t'ings?"

"Runnings a lickle slow right now."

Lancey picked up a cigarette, offered one but in vain. He lit up.

"Yes man, everyt'ing slow up yah." Then he asked, unsympathetically, "Your bwoy still in hospital?"

D. nodded slowly. Lancey shook his head and looked D. straight for a brief moment.

"Yuh find out who do it?"

D. smiled a little and shrugged.

"Yuh know how dis business go, Lancey. Ev'rybody make enemies." Then he said, "But you mus' know, since yuh ah police."

Lancey forced a laugh, not very heartily. D. grinned at him. Lancey pulled on his cigarette, he seemed to be looking for an angle. He looked at D. again.

"Is dat I did wan' see yuh about... privately, yuh know?"

D. knew what he meant. He opened up his arms outstretched.

"Yuh can talk Lancey, dem man deh is my family. Dem safe."

That didn't seem to please Lancey, but there wasn't much he could do about it. It was obvious neither of the two men trusted each other. Lancey nodded thoughtfully. He seemed preoccupied now.

"Well," he started, "you're right, I know who do it. An' you mus' know too. But hear wha'ppen: de bwoy ah work fe de police."

Lancey waited for D.'s reaction. There was none. After a pause D. said simply:

"Ah so dis business run, pure informer out deh." Then he asked, "Who tell yuh 'bout dis place?"

Once again Lancey laughed. D. smiled, he didn't expect an answer. He got back to the matter at hand.

"Dat cyan stop me, y'know."

Lancey paused before answering.

"Dem type ah situation kinda sensitive, yuh see. De bwoy payin' de police, so dem lookin' after him."

"Ev'rybody 'ave a price," D. said unimpressed, then added, "So yuh cyan really help me wid dat problem, Lancey."

It was a statement more than a question. Lancey finished his cigarette and stretched to stub it out in the ashtray on the desk.

D. had taken the initiative and intended to keep it.

"Tell me somet'ing," he asked. "Is what yuh really do fe de English police dem? I mean, dem pay yuh, right? So yuh mus' do some work fe dem..."

It was a loaded question, Lancey knew that. He grinned.

"Dem seh me is a 'consultant'."

He stressed the word as if he found it funny. Undeterred, D. repeated:

" 'Consultant', dat is someone who advise people, help dem ina dem work, nuh true?"

He didn't wait for confirmation.

"So really, is only 'bout we as Yard man yuh can advise dem."

It was indisputable logic. Lancey frowned and thought a little bit before answering.

"Yuh see me D., me a Yard man. Me coulda nevah defen' a foreigner 'gainst another Yard man."

D. looked at Lancey curiously.

"Bwoy, people ah tell me seh yuh ah mash up man runnins all over de place, ah pressure dem fe money an' t'ings like dat."

Lancey was studying D. closely.

"To tell yuh de trut'," D. continued, "me cyan stand up fe a nex' man business, but I know seh yuh couldn't ask me fe anyt'ing."

He left the statement hanging in the air. Lancey wasn't smiling much anymore.

"Every man haffe live, even police. Yuh know dat, man," he said seriously.

D. agreed.

"Police haffe live, yeah. Mek I show yuh somet'ing; I don't disrespeck no police as such, y'know Lancey. If a man choose to join de police, ah fe him business dat."

D. paused a little before dropping the counteraction.

"But I don't feel seh it right fe police fe get involve wid runnins and t'ings. Police haffe clean, man... Adderwise, who can yuh trust?"

He smiled. Pablo smiled at D.'s last remark too. It was a good joke but Lancey didn't really appreciate it. The conversation seemed to have sobered him up. It was now cards on the table. He cleared his throat.

"Look man, me jus' come look fe yuh, in case we coulda work an arrangement, seen?"

"What arrangement yuh ah talk 'bout?" D. asked. "Arrangement is a t'ing whe' two sides gain from it. But yuh cyan do notin' fe me."

Lancey fixed him with a long stare. He sighed.

"All me ah seh, dere's goin' to be a crackdown 'pon ouno, so if yuh smart you'd get on the right side."

Shaking his head, D. told Lancey:

"The right side? Everyt'ing me have me work fe it. Nobody nevah gimme notin'. So I look after myself de best I can. But I nuh gwine mek no deal wid no police, white or black. I rather dead than turn informer, see me."

That was telling it like it was. D. was in no mood to compromise with Lancey. Now less than ever. The policeman was getting increasingly frustrated, it had started to show.

"Alright," he said, "it look like yuh don't need my help."

D. squinted.

"Help? Hold on, mek I ask yuh somet'ing. Fe years you nevah stop run me down, an' if I nevah smart I woulda gone long time. How come yuh wan' help me now?"

You could see that Lancey was fast losing restraint. Pablo and Slinga could feel it but remained silent and cool in their corners. Lancey straightened up in his chair, his hands flat on his knees. His eyes were hard when he said:

"Watcha now, yuh don't wan' diss me."

It was almost a threat. D. kissed his teeth contemptuously, his hands flat on the desk, he looked straight at Lancey.

"Diss you?! Gwan go suck yuh mudda."

There couldn't be any stronger insult. Lancey leapt forward, but he never quite made it to the desk. He found himself staring down the barrel of the steel-grey automatic in Pablo's hand. Slinga stepped up from the back also, just in case. Lancey read the resolve in Pablo's stare and sat back down. He nodded throughtfully, his features contracted, visibly keeping a lid on his fury. D. shook his head. He had not moved an inch.

"Yuh losin' your temper, Lancey. Yuh use to be cooler than dat."

"T'ink I bettah leave," Lancey growled.

"Yeah man, go back to yuh friend dem."

Lancey got up slowly, under the vigilante gaze of the two soldiers.

"Yuh still de sherriff...?" D. asked him.

He was alluding to Lancey's boast during their encounter at the hospital. Lancey looked down at him but didn't answer. D. smiled.

"...Then 'member one t'ing: me is Bob Marley."

Lancey and the two soldiers were only too familiar with the song by the late reggae king to which D. was refering. The soldiers laughed at their boss' wit, Lancey didn't. He turned and started to walk off, buttoning his jacket on the way. Behind him, D. called out.

"Hey Lancey, one more t'ing; try an' dress bettah than dat man, unless is church yuh ah go!"

Pablo snickered. Even Slinga grinned in Lancey's face as he opened the door. D. motioned to Pablo to see Lancey off the premises. Slinga closed the door behind them. D. sighed and sat silent for a while. Then he told Slinga:

"Time longer than rope, my yout'. "

Laconically, Slinga nodded.

"Dirty babylon..."

Early Monday morning, Sweetie's phone call woke D. up. Jenny handed him the phone then departed with Jesse; they were late. D. listened, said he'd be right over and hung up. He got ready and drove to Sweetie's.

The journey was fraught with morning traffic, but D. showed no impatience. He hardly noticed the cars or the rush of pedestrians on their way to work. A timid sun was slowly soaking up the previous night's rain.

The car was silent; the stereo switched off. Sweetie opened almost as soon as he rang the bell. She got him to sit on the coach. D. didn't want any breakfast but she made him a hot drink anyway. The house was quiet, Leon had already left for school. From next door, a young baby's cry filtered through. After sipping some tea D. asked about Bess' whereabouts. She was upstairs. Sweetie's eyes locked into D.'s for a brief moment.

"What happen?" he asked.

Calmly, in a hollow voice, Sweetie explained that they'd gone to the hospital early, after dropping Leon off at school. When they got there, she said, she knew right away from the look on the nurse's face. They spoke with the doctor who explained that Linton had regained consciousness for a brief moment around 3am in the night, then had apparently suffered a massive heart attack. They had tried everything to revive him but eventually lost him. The doctor offered his condolences and left Sweetie and Bess in the hospital corridor. They simply left and drove back home. Bess had stayed in her room ever since, just sitting there, staring, her open Bible in front of her.

D. rubbed his face wearily. His brain felt numb after the flood of thoughts that had followed the news of Linton's death. It had been a possibility but D. had been optimistic. He and Sweetie remained silent for what seemed like a long time. Each lost in a meditation of their own. D. sighed and rose from the couch.

"Come, let's check Bess."

Sweetie got up and they climbed the stairs.

Bess answered the knock on the door, they went in. She was sitting exactly where Sweetie had left her some time before, one hand on the Bible. Her eyes were dry, staring somewhere beyond the window pane. She turned and got up as she saw D. and went to hug him. D. embraced her, his arms around her slender shoulders. He held her for a moment.

"It will be alright", he told Bess.

She let go of him and sat back down. D. and Sweetie sat on the bed beside her.

"Dem seh him regain consciousness," Bess said.

D. didn't quite know what to say. Linton was gone and he felt it.

"Jus' fe a little while." It was left to Sweetie to answer Bess.

"Nobody heard his last words..."

It was a strange statement, but Bess seemed concerned about that fact.

"Him 'ave family on yah?" Sweetie asked.

D. shook his head.

"We haffe sen' him home," Bess said softly.

"I will tek care of dat, man, don't worry about it," D.

reassured her.

A little ray of sunshine pierced its way through the shifting clouds and illuminated the small room. D. and the two women were each lost in their own thoughts. Bess turned to D.

"Him jus' turn twenty-four, yuh know. Me an' him born same month."

"Yuh jus' pray fe him, Bess, I'll deal wid de matter."

That was all D. could say. He felt unequipped to say anything philosophical at such a moment.

"D., yuh mus' let me help you, yuh understan'?"

D. stared down in front of him. He knew what Bess meant.

"Don't worry yuhself, everyt'ing programmed."

"D..." Bess started again.

D. got up.

"Bess, listen man, you res' yuhself today. Tomorrow, I come down and we sort it out, seen?"

Bess' dark eyes stared deep into his for a second then he turned and left the room. Sweetie followed him downstairs. D. told her to make the arrangements for Linton and get back to him later. Before going out he added:

"Yuh stay wid her, mek sure she alright."

"Nuh worry man, she be alright. She young but her spirit strong. I call yuh later."

"Call Charlie..." D. told her

Once D. had left, Sweetie went back upstairs to sit with Bess. She found her toying with a ring.

"Linton gimme it, fe my birt'day..." Bess said.

"Bess, I know how yuh feel. Linton was nice an' me grieve fe him. But yuh mus' stay strong. D. gwan mek sure dem fly him out an' bury him back home."

Bess listened but she was following her own train of thoughts.

"Yuh know somet'ing, Sweetie? I knew he wouldn't make it."

Sweetie looked at her.

"But yuh pray over him at the hospital every day..."

Bess nodded slowly.

"I had to pray fe him, but God know, I did know seh him was nevah gwine lef' dat bed."

Sweetie couldn't figure it out. She knew Bess had been a very spiritual person from an early age.

"Me jinxed yuh know, Sweetie. "

"Wha' yuh ah deal wid? Don't talk dem weh deh."

"Nah man, me ah tell yuh. De same t'ing happen again," Bess insisted.

"How yuh mean?"

"Yuh 'member Melvin?"

Sweetie realised what Bess meant, but didn't want her friend thinking like that.

"These t'ings happen, Bess. Dem man tek certain risk fe mek dem money."

"Me know Sweetie, but after dem kill Melvin I nevah even talk to a man, until I come up here an' meet Linton."

Sweetie knew Bess had been deeply affected by the killing of her first boyfriend at a dance in Toronto. It had taken her a few years to get over it. Now, with this other tragedy, Bess was taking it personally.

"I know, man. But don't t'ink like dat."

Bess looked at her.

"I'll be alright. Today I jus' cool right here an' pray. Tomorrow reaction start."

Sweetie could see the determination on Bess' face.

"D. don't wan' nobody to move until him ready," she said.

"Tomorrow, me an' you mek a little move, Sweetie."

Sweetie didn't answer. After a while she left Bess to herself.

The young woman needed time to come to terms with her loss. Sweetie cooked and ate a little. Despite Sweetie's insistence, Bess refused to eat anything.

After leaving Sweetie's house, D. drove around, unsure exactly where he was going. It was one thing to cope with his own grief but to see sorrow on a woman's face somehow brought home to him the real pain of the loss. Eventually he ended up at the house in Leyton where he found Slinga cleaning up his new guns in front of the television. The soldier took in the news, but did not comment on it. He wanted to hear what was on D.'s mind.

He put the guns away and waited patiently until...

"No more waiting; payback time now..."

D. had spoken to himself almost. He wasn't even looking in Slinga's direction but the soldier nevertheless repeated, "Payback, yes."

D. studied him and knew that he was thinking of Sticks. When Slinga heard of Sticks' killing on his return from the States, he waited as D. had ordered. But Sticks' death had upset him. Sticks was a man who had done everything for him as Slinga saw it. It was Sticks who had brought him in the business and showed him how to operate. And he wasn't about to forget that.

A litttle after midday, Puggy walked in. He had slipped out earlier and gone to the studio to finish work on a track from the previous week. Slinga told him what had happened and right away the young singer forgot all about his record. The three of them sat quietly.

"We gwan settle the score now?" Puggy asked finally
D. had meditated sufficiently on that.

"I want everyt'ing planned, no carelessness..." he said slowly.

"What about Lancey?" Slinga asked.

Somewhere in there Lancey was part of the problem. D. knew he would do his best to take him down now. He nodded.

"I have to deal wid him, before him try dus' me."

After that nothing much else was said about the matter. D. built a spliff and meditated by himself while Slinga watched cricket distractedly on cable TV. West Indies were thrashing England in a one day test, but today victory didn't taste sweet.

Puggy got up and decided to cook. A couple of hours later, he served up large plates of food and brought them over. D. refused at first, but Puggy insisted that he needed to eat. Later that afternoon, Pablo came over. He had already heard about Linton from Charlie. As evening drew near, D. sent Puggy to buy some stout, beer, a bottle of rum plus some rizla. Several hours through, the four men sat with the drinks, reasoning and talking stories from the past. It seemed like a kind of wake, a sending-off the way they all felt it had to be done. After the initial sadness, their feeling changed to a different vibe which, fueled a little by the liquor, helped each one to gain comfort from the loss and strength for the days to come. Linton got his salute, as was his due.

Later again, Pablo and Puggy left for the Spot. Business had to keep running, come joy or pain. D. and Slinga had one more drink. The bottle of rum had been distressed but neither of them was a 'bad' rum drinker. D. lit up a spliff, sprawled across the sofa, shoes off, shirt open, taking in the sounds from the cassette, but his mind high up. Slinga across in the chair was feeling much the same way. None of them paid attention to the late news bulletin. They had had all the news they needed for one day. D. had gone to the bathroom when the phone rang. He heard Slinga calling him.

"Who dat?!" D asked, washing his hands

"Sherry!" Slinga shouted over the music.

D. took some water in cupped hands and splashed it on his face. In the mirror his eyes squinted back at him. He breathed in deeply and turned away to pick up a towel.

"I cyan see her," he said, walking back to the living room. He simply didn't feel in the mood to be nice, not tonight. But Sherry insisted on talking to him. He took the call and she sensed right away that D. was on a strange vibe. She wanted to see him anyway, maybe she couldn't help, but she wanted to be close. Sherry promised she'd leave if he really didn't want her there. She said she'd take a taxi.

D. replaced the receiver, realising he had not tried too hard to keep her away. He knew why. Times like these when he felt close to death, somehow a woman's presence always made him hang tight to life. Tomorrow, he would have to be hard, cold and do what was right, regardless of the cost. Tonight, he was still alive and needed to feel that way.

They say that bad news never comes alone...

When his phone rang at dawn on Tuesday morning, D. almost ignored it. He didn't know what time Sherry had gone home, but his head was heavy and his body crying out for more rest. Jenny's first words hit him like an ice cold shower.

"D., they just raided the house!"

He was stunned speechless. Jenny sounded shaken as she explained that the police had only just left her flat. They were looking for him, two of them had guns and the black policeman from the hospital was also with them...

"Hold on, hol' on..."

D. thought of something.

"Yuh alright? Jesse alright?"

"Yeah we're okay, but..."

"Listen, hang up now, go to Carol after work, yuh understan'? Hang up the phone. Later!"

D. cut the call short. The police might just be bugging the house. Several things raced through his mind. Lancey... Lancey was out for him. He had expected him to try something, but not like this.

'Dat dog ah use de police dem, said way...' D. thought, as he jumped off the bed. Suddenly he realised that had it not been for Sherry, he would have gone home to Jenny. He scratched his head, standing in the middle of the room in his shorts. Outside, it was just about daylight. Lancey...

D.'s mind kept coming back to him. He swore, went to the bathroom and showered rapidly. The downpour of lukewarm water refreshed him. He washed as the situation worked its way around in his head the whole time. This was war! It was typical of Lancey's mentality. He couldn't face D. man to man. He was a police, when it suited him. D. was not a man to hate; whatever he had done, it was never through hatred. Even revenge was for honour, but hate was never involved. Yet as he dried himself with the towel he knew that, police or not, Lancey was going to pay. One thought kept flashing through D.'s mind.

'Him bring gun over my yout'!'

This time, that was it.

D. went back to his room and dressed quickly, trying all the time to keep thinking clearly. Slinga emerged from the next room, yawning, on his way to the toilet.

"Wha'ppen, don?" he asked.

"Him fuck himself now!"

Slinga straightened up.

"Wha' ah gwan?"

"Lancey an' de police dem jus' raid my yard."

"Wha'!"

D. explained what he knew. Slinga stood there, taking in the situation.

"Anyhow you'da gone home las' night, yuh gone!" he said.

D. nodded.

"Dat mean seh dem ah search de place fe yuh."

Slinga was right. The police raid had been a failure but Lancey would be out there looking for him personally.

"I wonder if any bwoy know dis place?" D. said.

"Which place, yahso?"

Slinga thought about it. The house might still be safe for the time being, but Lancey would be looking for anyone who could lead him to D.

"I gwan call Charlie."

D. went for the phone in the living room.

"Whe' Puggy deh?"

"Him ah sleep," Slinga said.

D. called Charlie and explained what had happened. Charlie said he should stay put, for the time being anyway. D. asked him to call Pablo at his house, then hung up the phone. Puggy woke up shortly after and was quickly filled in on what had happened. D. had some tea but didn't feel for no food. Puggy and Slinga had breakfast. The three men all stayed in, discussing the options. D. was working out what his next move should be. He knew this was showtime, and he wasn't running but he wanted it to be his show. Once he had checked out every possible play, evaluated his chances, he relaxed. The dice were rolling and he might as well stop worrying; that's the way he saw it. He tried calling overseas around 1pm, but the lines were temporarily out.

About the same time, Pablo was parking his car at the back alongside the school. He locked it and walked down the bright, sunny street. He felt extremely hungry and hoped it was oxtail stew day at GBs. Alternatively he would settle for chicken but his stomach was crying out. After leaving D. the previous night, he had gone to the Spot and stayed there until closing time, as usual around 5.30 am. After that he had driven Vera home, instead of putting her in a cab. Vera was okay, but Pablo didn't like her coming to the club too often. Whenever she hadn't seen him for a week or so, as sometimes happened, she would come all the way from Lewisham to catch him at the Spot. Pablo didn't feel like seeing her last night, particularly after the bad vibe of Linton's death. Yet he ended up staying in south London with her, and now he felt hungry.

In front of the restaurant, a few youths were eating and chatting. A girl on her way out said, "Hi," as Pablo pushed the door open. He returned the greeting, wondering where he knew her from. It was oxtail stew day after all and Pablo got some served up rapidly.

His food in hand, he stepped outside to eat in the sun. August had begun warmly, continuing a run of almost three months of good weather.

Pablo leaned against the wall to the right of the restaurant window and got busy on the oxtail and rice. To his right some youths were talking. A little further by the kerbside, a dreadlocks was chatting up a pretty girl standing by his car. The food was hot and spicy, Pablo was enjoying it to the max.

Across the road, on the right hand side, two men parked in a brown car were observing him. One was young, slim, blond with a chequered shirt. He was the driver. His companion, his passenger at any rate, was larger, dark-skinned and wearing shades. He wasn't very talkative and had more or less ignored his colleague's attempts at conversation all morning. To his great disappointment, the dawn raid had failed to catch the man he wanted and now they had stuck him with this idiot and his cockney accent. Lancey was vexed, there was no other way to describe it. He knew the man had been sent to keep an eye on him, that was annoying him even more. But there, across the road, he could see someone he wanted almost as much as D. Eventually, Lancey convinced the white policeman to step out of the car and check the man out. They started out together towards the restaurant. It wasn't long before they'd been made out. Nobody moved but Lancey could feel the stares. Pablo had been alerted by one of the youths next to him. He knew deep inside as soon as he saw him, that Lancey was coming for him. But Pablo was no fool, he knew Lancey's ways and calculated very quickly that he had one chance, but only if he stayed cool. The two police moved in closer, everyone stood up watching them. Pablo continued eating, chewing the food leisurely, apparently oblivious to the two men. He stared blankly in Lancey's direction though, waiting. The young white police was a little bit in front coming his way. Pablo stopped eating suddenly, his plastic fork up in the air, the young police was within reach now. He took a badge out of his pocket and said something about "CID". Lancey was about to come level. Pablo reacted quickly. All in one movement, he threw his food container straight into the white police's face and pushed him with all his strength onto Lancey coming up behind. Then he took off, fast. Lancey took the full impact of the white police falling, yet brushed him away forcefully with his left arm. He had expected some kind of reaction from the youth but this fool got in the way. The white police fell to one side, trying to regain his balance. Meanwhile, Lancey had reached in his waist, pulled out a gun and was taking aim at the sprinting Pablo, barely fifteen yards away. A girl cried out, "Oh my God!" The wiser youths in front of the restaurant all got down low, trying their best to duck from any stray bullets. It was the white police officer who saved Pablo. He was back on his feet and dived onto Lancey, pushing up his gun hand. The shot rang out, loud and dry, buzzed less than two feet above Pablo's head. The youth didn't even turn, but continued at full speed until finally disappearing from sight around the bend. Lancey tried to follow him, but the white officer was determined and stood right in front of him. Lancey took off his shades and for a few short seconds considered thumping him. But he cursed instead, only just managing to restrain himself.

"That's not the way we do things around here," the white police officer was saying, out of breath. Lancey marched off back towards the car, the other officer following him. The bemused and shaken little crowd on the scene were soon joined by the others from inside GBs and a loud debate ensued, the survivors pointing to the brown, unmarked police car speeding away in the distance.

Once around the corner, Pablo kept on pushing, right across the road into the side street leading to the row of factories and garages. Quickly he opted right, sprinted down the alley and turned into the main road. He'd heard the loud bang behind him and, as they say, fear gives man wings... Pablo knew they were likely to search the area and once the radio call had gone through, it would be hell to escape. His luck came in when a passing bus had to slow down at the lights to allow for turning cars. Pablo caught his breath and only just made it to the bus as it started picking up speed. With agility, he jumped onto the platform and ran upstairs. As he sat on one of the empty seats, keeping low, he slowly recovered his breath. He wasn't sure where the bus was heading; he didn't care either. He had just heard death whistling close, too close, to his head. Now he was angry.

"De bloodclaat bwoy try murder me!" he swore under his breath, still shocked. A cold anger started to consume him. Pablo looked up and heard the controller.

"Where you goin', mate?"

Still blowing out air, he searched his pockets for change.

D. didn't eat, smoke or drink that day. He felt cool though, clear-headed. He felt like making a move around 6.30pm so he asked Slinga to call a minicab. He thought it wiser to leave his too-visible car at home. D. and Slinga left, reaching Carol's house around nightfall. Her son Damian opened up for them. Jesse was in the hallway, he ran to his father. Venetta, Carol's daughter, came out.

"Oh hi D., Mum, it's D!"

D. accompanied the children into the living room, Jesse touched Slinga's fist and followed his father. Jenny was sitting in the kitchen where Carol was fixing dinner for the children. D. and Slinga paused outside the kitchen. The first thing D. saw were his wife's unsmiling eyes glaring at him.

"Wha'ppen Carol?" he asked.

"Nothing, what happen?" she said looking at him. "Alright," she answered Slinga's greeting.

D. turned to Jenny.

"Wha' yuh ah seh, Jen?"

Jenny paused a little.

"Wha' me ah seh?" she repeated. Then, as calmly as she could. "Can you tell me what's happening?"

D. sighed. Slinga had gone to sit in the living room.

"Then yuh nuh know wha'ppen? Dat police bwoy out fe me."

Carol looked at him from the stove.

"That guy looks like bad news," she said.

D. didn't answer.

"So, what happen?" he asked.

Jenny had to go through the whole thing. D. listened, then asked a few questions.

"Is he after you in particular?" Carol asked.

D. sneered.

"Yeah, me one. Ah my personal police, yuh know."

Jenny didn't share his sense of humour.

"You find that funny? Police dragged me out of my bed, and my son... your son..."

D. knew if he didn't stop her now the recriminations would be lengthy.

"Watcha now: nuh budda wid dat, y'hear? I don't need it, not now, seen?"

Jenny stayed silent but still looked upset.

"I know yuh vex 'bout dat," D. told her, "but right now I need to t'ink, fast, else me gone, yuh understan'?"

Jenny shook her head.

"Why is he after you, what have you done to him?"

D. was almost surprised at the question.

163

"Me? Notin', notin' at all..."

"What does he want you for?" Carol asked him.

D. looked at her and said simply:

"Money."

"Money?" Carol repeated.

D. nodded. In simple terms, that was it. Carol couldn't believe it.

"So you mean, he comes all the way from Jamaica to ask you for money?!" she asked.

D. let out a short bitter laugh.

"Yeah... Ev'rybody want to get paid."

"How much money?" Jenny asked.

D. looked at her.

"What d'you mean 'how much money'?"

He hadn't even thought about that.

"How much does he want?" Jenny repeated.

"Look man, money is not de problem. The point is, I don't pay no police, yuh understan' me?"

"They're all at it," Carol said.

She started picking up plates and served the food. Then she called the children, sending back those who rushed in without washing their hands first.

"Let's leave them," she said.

D. and Jenny went to sit in the living room, where Slinga was watching a programme on TV, at least he seemed to be.

"Would you like a drink, D.?" Carol asked.

D. declined, Slinga said he was cool. Carol sat down opposite them. D. and Jenny shared the couch.

"I'm not going home tonight..." Jenny said. "I'm staying here for a few days."

"You're going to have to go away, until this cools down," Carol said.

D. looked at her.

"It nah go cool down."

"What do you mean? He must have other people to chase, no?"

"This is personal now," D. explained.

Slinga spoke.

"De bwoy try diss de don!"

"Is he the one who shot your friend?" Carol asked.

"By the way, how is Linton?" Jenny turned to D.

It was only then that D. realised he had not seen Jenny since... He caught Slinga's brief gaze. D.'s face was blank when he said matter-of-factly:

"Linton dead, y'know..."

"What?! When?!" a shocked Carol asked.

Jenny gasped and closed her eyes. No one said anything for several seconds. Then D. briefly explained what he knew. Jenny looked even more shaken now.

"Was it him?" Carol asked.

D. shook his head.

"It's not dat man; de bwoy wan' kill me long time."

"This is never gonna stop, is it?" Jenny said somberly. She went on. "It's going to go on and on, until..."

D. knew his woman. She could say the most awkward things at the most awkward times. He couldn't take that tonight.

"Look Jen, I don't wan' hear dem t'ings, seen?! Notin' ah go gwan on an' on. I gwan stop it now."

Jenny looked at him.

"Stop it? You?!"

"Wha' yuh ah deal wid?"

"You can't stop it, there'll always be someone after you."

D. frowned and kissed his teeth. He turned to Carol.

"Is why she haffe gwan dem way deh, cho'!"

165

"She's scared," Carol told him.

Jenny cut back in.

"What about your son, you don't even think about him."

D. was trying resolutely to keep calm. Why did she have to be so ignorant?"

"Look man, if yuh don't have notin' positive fe say, don't talk to me." He paused. "Yuh nuh see seh my life at stake!"

"It's always been, that's the way you live."

"Jenny, jus' cool down, okay." Carol exercised a little sisterly authority. "What are you planning to do?" she asked D.

"I gwan deal wid him."

"But he is a police, D."

Slinga's voice cut in, sharp.

"Him dirty, man!"

D. seemed determined and didn't really see Carol's distinction. He turned to his sister-in-law.

"Yuh see me, Carol, I don't come up yah fe fun. I have to mek a life an' mek money, so dat my yout' don't grow up poor like how I grow. Anybody try stop dat, dead." He added, "I never set out fe live long, but I determined to live good."

"If you touch that guy more police will come for you," Carol warned.

"Not if I do it neatly."

Carol couldn't see how.

An idea was fermenting in D.'s head.

"I am not crazy, y'know, I learn a lot of t'ings 'bout dis game." He paused. "Yuh see de way 'nuff Yardman come up yah an' start run business, dem don't like it. De whole t'ing is about power. Because once we get all dat money, we too big. We nuh suppose to 'ave dat."

Carol was listening.

"That's true, but once you've got that what do you do?" she

166

asked.

"Well, then you can live bettah. Is only poor people who get no choice. Ev'rybody wan' bettah clothes, bettah house, bettah schools an' everyt'ing. But widout money, yuh cyan get to it."

Carol agreed.

"What about the drugs though, D.? You know it's hurting us. As long as we keep killing each other over that, we'll never get organised."

D. reflected a little.

"Yuh see drugs...? Alright, remember when we used to grow herb ah Yard, an' pay light bills an' water rate an' buy t'ings wid the money... When de big bwoys dem see dat, dem seh 'poor black people ah get money, dem ah look after demselves!' So dem bring soldier an' helicopter come burn down de plantations."

"Yeah I remember that," Carol said.

"Is right after dat dem bring in de drugs, yuh know. An' from dat, every yout' want a way outta de ghetto get involve. Too much money ina dat..."

Carol sighed.

"We're losing a lot of youngsters to that."

D. nodded.

"We need opportunities, Carol. Until then, it's drugs will run t'ings. De rich want to stay rich, we nuh 'ave notin' to lose..."

The conversation seemed to be going in circles, right and wrong blending intangibly. Finally, Jenny cut in.

"I saw Soni today."

"Yeah, she alright?" he asked.

"She's okay, but she's gonna have the baby early."

Since Soni had been in and out of hospital throughout her pregnancy, it was to be expected. Since Sticks' death, Jenny had kept in contact with Soni, helping her with advice and anything else the best she could. She had grown to like her and Soni had changed a lot since also.

"Remind me about her later," D. said.

He had regularly given Jenny money for his late friend's woman. The mention of Soni now reminded him of the immediate situation.

Carol was in the kitchen, checking on the children.

"Tell me somet'ing, sis?" D. called to her. "Nah de social service yuh work for?"

"That's right," Carol said, as she maintained order in the kitchen.

D. was pursuing an idea.

"Ouno can find out t'ings 'bout people, don't?"

Carol laughed.

"Well sometimes, but it's confidential."

D. saw Slinga looking his way. The youth was always very sharp, seemingly detached but ever on the alert, and he had to be. D. nodded and got up.

"Show me somet'ing."

He stepped into the kitchen...

D. and Slinga stayed at Carol's until 9.30pm. Jenny followed her husband into the passage while Jesse was busy testing his boxing skills on Slinga.

"I'll go back home on Friday," Jenny said.

"Alright, jus' cool yah so wid your sister. An' stop worrying."

"I can't stop worrying. People keep getting shot around you, I'm scared for you."

D. sighed and shook his head. He looked at his wife. He touched her face with his hand and smiled.

"Yuh musn't t'ink like dat. I will sort it out. Jus' look after my bwoy."

Jenny was visibly upset.

"Yuh comin' here tomorrow?"

"Yeah man, evenin' time."

Carol called out as they left:

"I'll try D., but I can't promise."

D. grabbed Jesse and raised him above his head.

"Later, rude bwoy."

The little boy giggled. Slinga said 'later' and followed D. out to a waiting cab.

Puggy was still home. He told D. Charlie had been trying to contact him but apparently his mobile was not working properly. D. called Charlie but Charmaine answered. She said Charlie had just left with Pablo. D. tried Charlie's mobile...

Charlie had called the meeting for 7pm. The atmosphere was subdued, heavy, the riddim track bouncing out of the stereo as by habit. The feeling was altogether different from what it used to be. Not much drinking or smoking was going on tonight. Each man now knew everything about the situation at hand. The whole thing was at risk, and something had to be done fast. As always Charlie appealed for calm and a concrete plan as opposed to rash action. In his corner, Pablo was still seething from the incident of the previous day. For him there was no two ways about it; Lancey had to go down. Slinga was a little calmer but he had made his position clear earlier: "Kill dem all!" He was only waiting on D.'s word.

Seated across from Charlie, D. seemed strangely detached from the whole thing tonight. He had told Charlie that it was now either or either; unless they could find a way to eliminate Lancey, the business was over. As for their other enemies, he was determined to settle that account also. Charlie loooked around the room, he had been meditating all night, hardly sleeping, reviewing all aspects of the problem. He knew D. was absolutely right.

"What's your plan?" he asked.

"I have a plan," D. said looking at him, "but... I need two plan."

"Two plans?!"

"Yeah. Is two problems we 'ave to solve. Me have somet'ing line up fe de first one, but is Lancey's problem me ah work 'pon."

"Can we set him up?" Charlie asked.

D. looked at him.

"Set him up?"

"Check this out; he's dirty, right? Is there any way we can set him up for a fall? That way they'll send him back."

D. frowned as he considered Charlie's idea.

"Him haffe dead," Pablo said determinedly "Notin' less."

Slinga waited silently.

"Charlie, anyhow him get out alive him will come back fe me, I know dat," D. explained.

Charlie shook his head.

"I don't like when we start talkin' about smokin' cops, you know what I'm sayin'?"

D. looked unperturbed. He squinted.

"Cop? Him is jus' a fraud, he jus' gets paid."

"Maybe he does," Charlie said, "but if we 'off' him, that's it, it's never gonna go away."

Charlie continued pressing his point. He looked gloomy.

"What d'you think they brought him here for? He knows most of the people operating over here. They know they can't stop the business their way but they think a man like him could get the job done."

D. was thinking about it for a while. He pointed out to Charlie:

"But dat guy's worse than dem, him tek everywhere."

Charlie picked up his spliff from the ashtray with a little laugh. He lit it.

"That's why. By the time he's finished he'll have everything and everybody under control. First, he's setting us one against the other, think about it..."

The smoke drifted around Charlie's head. D.tapped a rhythm on the arm of the chair. He scratched the back of his head.

"You're right."

Charlie nodded.

"There must be a way, yuh know... No trace..."

Charlie was thinking about it. Slinga and Pablo were silent. Everyone was feeling more or less the same vibe. Then the bell rang and Charmaine opened the door to let Sweetie and Bess in. The women greeted everyone and sat down.

D. was looking at Bess. She seemed serious but not sad. Still, there wasn't much her almond-shaped dark eyes revealed about her state of mind.

"D. we 'ave somet'ing," Sweetie said.

D. listened. Sweetie explained that she and Bess had baited Glenda the previous night through her cousin. When she got to the flats, expecting a few smokes and an offer of a job from some alleged player, Bess and Sweetie held onto her and marched her back to their car. Sweetie had explained that they were after Simon, apparently ignoring the girl's role in the affair. They told her that it was becoming known that Simon wanted her out because she was a 'weak' link... The girl was terrified. She said that since the shooting she had been living at her mother's and had not been back to the club. When Bess

171

pressured her she admitted speaking to Simon on the phone two days earlier. She was nevertheless only too ready to believe what the two women had had to say. She knew Simon was capable of wiping her out and literally began shaking. She was so terrified that she would have probably co-operated even without the gift of a couple of rocks and the promise of some money. An hour later, Sweetie and Bess released a sweating Glenda.

D. nodded and looked at the two women.

"Ouno dangerous, man."

Everyone agreed with that.

"Tell me somet'ing, yuh nuh feel seh she gwan tell de bwoy?"

Sweetie shook her head. We give her what she needs, him don't response fe her no more."

"What about the police?" Charlie asked.

"Police is not looking for who shot Linton, or Sticks, yuh know dat. De bwoy whe' do it work fe dem."

That was very true and summed up the whole situation in this respect. Sweetie added:

"Anyway, Bess tell de gal seh, anyhow she talk to anybody, she dead. She believe dat."

D. glanced towards Bess. The girl was sitting quietly, listening. He knew it had taken a lot for her not to hurt Glenda.

"So we know where the guy lives," Charlie said. "What are you thinking about?"

"We jus' ambush him," Slinga said calmly. D. wasn't totally against that but he was thinking ahead. He shook his head, not totally satisfied.

"Yuh know wha' me ah look for, Charlie; I want a nice set up, somet'ing clean... To kill two birds wid one stone."

The old proverb, as it were, suited the situation perfectly. Slinga smiled.

"Fe real...!"

"You're sure this Simon guy is paying Lancey, right?" Charlie asked.

D. nodded.

"Feel so, yuh know." Then he added, looking at Charlie, "I was jus' t'inking de same t'ing..."

Charlie smiled. They were both going down the same track. Charlie asked, smiling even wider:

"You wanna know what Lancey wants even more than money right now?"

D. squinted. "Me," he said.

D. didn't say anything else for a while. No one else did either. The general current of thought was about a set-up. When D. spoke to Charlie he came straight to the point, knowing that they were all with him.

"It can work... but we need perfect timing."

Charlie was still working the details of it in his mind.

"You don't want a shootout," he advised. "The best thing would be to get inside."

D. nodded. "Inside, yes."

The plan in D.'s mind kept shaping up, piece by piece, bit by bit. Once he had thought about it thoroughly, it sounded almost perfect. Charlie watched him closely, Pablo and Slinga also. After leaving him some time to think, Charlie winced.

"One thing though, that Simon guy probably can't get to Lancey to bring him there."

It was D.'s turn to smile, for the first time tonight.

"Yeah, but I know someone who can do dat..."

Charlie was trying to figure it out. It was Bess who pinpointed the one hitch.

"D., yuh still haffe get inside de yard."

D. looked at her.

"True, ah dat me want."

"I can do it."

D. looked at her seriously.

"You?"

"Yes man, I know I could get in."

Everyone, even Sweetie, was staring at Bess. They listened as she added:

"Look if I can get to him, I can play a part. That way you'll get him alone."

Sweetie was frowning. Slinga and Pablo were studying the slim woman thinking about what she was saying.

"Hey, he's not gonna fall for that, Bess," Charlie told her.

She didn't answer. D. asked:

"How yuh can do dat? 'Member seh, him ah look out fe we. Him will see t'rough dat."

"Not if I play it right."

It sounded crazy but Bess sounded sure of herself. Sweetie told her it would never work and the rest of the crew seriously disputed the scheme. For the next twenty miniutes, Bess explained her plan and defended it point by point. She knew if she could convince D. it just might work, that would be good enough. He was concerned for her safety, yet he had to admit it would be a smart move. Finally, after much hesitation he agreed that it was worth a shot, as long as the play was monitored properly. It sounded too good not to try it. If anything went wrong, they would have to improvise and that was where D. was concerned about Bess. But she was determined and Sweetie herself had also started believing in it. Before winding up the meeting, D. insisted that Pablo should leave town for a few days, until the problem was solved. Pablo protested but eventually had to obey the instructions given to him to go and check on the operations outside London. As he got up to leave, D. called out to Sweetie.

"I want yuh to get somebody number fe me..."

By Thursday afternoon, D. had been rehearsing the scheme in his mind a thousand times. There was an element of uncertainty in the plan but he felt it would work. That evening, he went to Carol's house to see his wife and son. Carol handed him a piece of folded paper. D. opened it and nodded thoughtfully: it was the address Bess and Sweetie had gotten from Glenda. Jenny was okay but wanted to know what D. was going to do. At the same time she knew he wouldn't tell her. Once again he reassured her then played with his son. D. didn't like the feeling of being in hiding. That wasn't his style, especially when the threat to his life was so direct. But he kept cool, coldly shaping in his mind the downfall of his enemies. That night, back at home, he called a number.

"Yeah!" someone answered.

It wasn't the voice he wanted so he said:

"I wan' speak to your boss."

"Who dis?"

"Tell him, D. deh 'pon de line."

Not too long after, another voice.

"Yaow!"

"Is me, man."

"D., wha' ah gwan? How yuh get my number?" Joseph asked, relaxed.

D. sneered down the line.

"I have spies in your house."

Joseph laughed. "So wha' yuh ah seh?"

175

"Hear wha'ppen; de bwoy deh 'pon de rampage. Yuh hear anyt'ing?"

"Dem seh 'nuff heat ah gwan 'round your side."

"Alright, certain t'ings gwan tek place. I need yuh fe do somet'ing fe me."

"Like... what kinda t'ing?" Joseph asked.

D. pointed out seriously:

"Hol' on, mek I show yuh somet'ing; dis is your problem too. After me deal wid him, yuh owe me, don't forget dat."

Joseph didn't contest the statement.

"So, yuh feel seh yuh can tek him?" he asked.

It was a genuine question.

"Somebody haffe do it," D. said. "So hear what I wan' yuh do. Yuh know where to reach him, nuh true?"

"Him ah deal wid a girl me control."

"Alright, tomorrow yuh check him, tell him seh one ah my soldier come to yuh. Tell him a deal ah go down Friday, somebody ah buy from me. Mek it sound like yuh want me out, yuh vex wid me from dem time, seen?"

Joseph was getting the picture. He asked again:

"Yuh need anyt'ing?"

"No, jus' convince him dat I gettin' set-up."

"Yuh sure seh him alone gwan come?"

D. laughed a little down the line.

"Lancey nuh crazy; from money an' stock deh deh, an' me deh deh too, him nah bring nobody."

Joseph said he would do it. D. arranged to call him back the next day with the time and the address. No use giving too much notice, he thought. He hung up. Then he picked up the receiver again. He put it back down then picked it up again and dialled a Kingston, Jamaica number. A female voice, rich and melodious, answered.

176

"Hello, good afternoon."

"Hello, can I speak to Skeets."

The woman had perfect diction.

"I'm afraid Mister Skeets is not in at the moment,"

"What time is he coming back?"

"He's had to go out of town, can I take a message?"

"Yeah, tell him... tell him, nah it's alright, I'll call back."

D. hung up without waiting for the answer. He waited a while then dialled another Kingston number. This time he got through straight away.

"Hello? Oh how are you doing? Yeah, hold on, I'll get her."

D. waited until he heard his woman's voice.

"Hi baby, what happen?"

"Everybody alright. How yuh stay?"

"Cool man, me alright."

"Yuh don't sound alright, wha' ah gwan?"

Donna knew him well enough to detect something in his voice.,

"Notin', I jus' tired."

"Then yuh nah res' properly? Is who tek 'way your strengt'?"

D. had to laugh.

"Nah man, how yuh always t'ink dem way. Right now, is certain problems I tryin' to deal wid."

"We comin' back Sunday," Donna said. *"Mek sure yuh come to the airport..."*

"Hol' on now."

D. waited. Donna came back on the line.

"Somebody wan' talk to yuh. Say 'hi' to your daddy."

"Hello, who is this?"

D. could hear Avril mumbling at the other end, Donna urging her to say something. The little voice came on.

"Daddy? Daddy?"

D. smiled, realising how much he had missed his daughter.

"Hi baby, what yuh doing?"

Avril said something and for a while D. tried to get her to talk. She was saying things but he couldn't catch much. Donna came back on.

"She try talk too fast!" she laughed.

"I don't send the money as yet," D. said. "I gwan do dat tomorrow."

"Alright, Leroy was here dis mornin'. Him seh fe tell yuh everyt'ing line up. Him gwan gimme de plans of de house fe yuh. Yuh eat today?"

D. didn't bother lying.

"Bwoy, I don't really feel hungry. "

Donna didn't like the sound of that.

"What happened to you, yuh nah res' an' yuh don't eat. Yuh wan' get sick?"

"Nah man, don't worry, I'll be alright."

"Hmmm, good t'ing me comin' back, is like yuh ah live bad, man."

Donna always worried about him. He felt like talking to her some more to ease up some of the things he kept inside, but he knew that she'd get too worked up. He remembered something he'd been meaning to ask.

"Donna, I wan' yuh do somet'ing fe me, before you leave."

"Wha'dat?"

"I wan' yuh go look for my daughta, leave some money fe her."

"Which part she live?" Donna asked.

D. gave her the address of the child's grandmother where she stayed.

"Tek Avril wid yuh, mek her know her sista," he added.

"Alright."

"Me love how you stay, yuh know Donna."

Donna knew what he meant.

"Then how yuh gimme so much problems?" she countered.

178

"Don't say dat, man."

"Fe real, D. Me ah worry 'bout yuh. Full time now yuh start cool down. Yuh takin' too much risk."

Everyt'ing is a risk in life, Donna. To mek it, a man mus' do de best he can."

"I don't care much about money, yuh know D. I jus' wan' live a peaceful life wid you an' de children. Yuh understan'?"

D. said he understood. He would work it out.

"What time de flight comin' in?" he asked.

"In the afternoon, three-thirty, we leavin' Saturday night."

"Alright, me come fe yuh. I sendin' de money tomorrow. Mek sure yuh go an' collect it."

Before he hung up, Donna told him:

"Don't forget; Sunday."

"How me fe forget?! Yuh tek care, right. Tell Avril me see her soon."

D. hung up.

He got up to switch off the main light and sat back down in semi-darkness. He stayed there for a long time, pictures floating in his head. The TV was turned down. Puggy was out, Slinga was in his room. Outside, only the odd passing car disturbed the quiet night. D. stretched on the couch and hit the 'off' button on the remote control. When he finally got to sleep it was almost dawn.

Around 10am, Charlie arrived and woke him up. D. went to shower while Charlie set up some tea. They both sat at the table. Charlie unfolded a flyer and laid it face down on the table. On the back was drawn a house plan showing two streets and a park. Charlie sipped some tea and waited a little.

"I been to check out the layout early this morning." He pointed on the paper. "That's the front, that's the back, with the

179

garage and garden. That's a tall fence. Here at the front there's a basement room with stairs going down. I guessed the other rooms at the back. There's a park with some trees, benches, but it's probably closed at night. The road is open both ways. The alley beside the garage is a dead-end."

D. listened, impressed. Charlie was an expert at this kind of thing, very thorough. D. explained what he planned to do and Charlie asked questions, pointing out possible weaknesses. After a while D. said:

"Yuh know somet'ing Charlie; all we ah plan, anyt'ing could go wrong still. We jus' try to mek it as safe as possible, but in any case de job 'ave to be done."

Charlie looked at his partner.

"Yeah, I know. But you make sure you get out of there on time."

D. smiled.

"How is Bess?"

"You know I thought you were crazy at first, but you just might be right. Sweetie told me about her, she says she's gotta lotta juice. You know what I'm saying?"

Coming from Sweetie this was high praise.

"Well everyt'ing ready den."

"You trust Joseph?" Charlie asked.

D. shrugged.

"No, but him depend 'pon me."

Charlie paused then pointed out:

"The timing has to be perfect D., otherwise... forget it."

D. knew that. He got up and stretched.

"Oh yeah, listen now, I want yuh to send some money ah Yard fe me."

He gave Charlie the necessary details. They agreed on the rest of the plans for later, then Charlie left just as Slinga was surfacing. D. went over the plans with him. Slinga asked a few questions but on the whole he thought like D.: follow the plan as far as it worked then if anything went wrong it would be all out rumpus.

"Still, I want it to go right, the set-up 'ave to work."

"Yes, don, we can mek it work."

The youth sounded confident.

The rest of the day went slow. The sun was back out after two greyish days. Puggy reappeared in the afternoon with a rough mix cassette of his latest tune. They played it several times then Puggy cooked and made sure that D. ate something... Then as the evening approached, D. went to lie down after giving instructions to be awoken at the right time. Puggy and Slinga started a ludo game.

D. got his call at 10pm as he had requested. He showered, picked some clothes and was soon ready. Puggy and Slinga were still trying to find out who was the 'baddest' at ludo. They had won an equal number of games and the current one seemed to be going to Slinga.

"Cho'!" Puggy exclaimed, as his opponent rolled another double 6 and pushed his last horse up.

Slinga did win eventually. He then got up and started to get ready.

"Puggy you stay right yahso, in case anyt'ing go wrong and we have to call in." D. told the young singer.

Puggy wasn't thrilled about that, he wanted to come along but said he would stay put. D. picked up his phone and took an extra battery. As he was slipping his shoes on, the phone rang.

He answered; it was Sherry. D. talked to her for a couple of minutes and said that he was busy, he would call tomorrow. He hung up and once again checked the details in his mind just in case he'd overlooked something, but all seemed to have been covered. Waiting for Slinga, he absent-mindedly picked up the ludo dice from the table and juggled them in the palm of his right hand. Slinga entered the room. D. threw down the dice: double 4. He turned and started out.

"Yuh ready?" D. asked inside the car.

Slinga nodded.

"Everyt'ing set," he answered.

The dashboard clock read 11.48.

D. drove out and headed for Islington. He wanted to be there well in advance, check out the scene carefully, get a feel of the place. When they got there he drove around twice, checked out the front, the side streets and the back; everything was as Charlie had mapped it. Then he and Slinga sat in the car on the road bordering the square, a little way past it, from where they could observe all traffic coming in. D. took out the automatic .44 which Sticks had given him on his return to London, the year before. He had cleaned it and loaded it earlier on. He rested the gun on the seat beside him, leaned back against the headrest and waited.

For lovers of soul, rare groove and swing beat, Satellite was the Friday night fixture. The design was inviting, the atmosphere relaxed and the more stylish girls in town always seemed to congregate there. A dozen or so of these were pressing their way in from outside, taking advantage of the last few minutes of the 'ladies free before midnight' policy. Most of the tables in the first lounge were already taken, the other smaller room after the bar had a little dancing crowd growing bigger all the time.

Sitting at the bar, Simon adjusted the designer tie around the collar of his Italian shirt. He ordered a second cognac. Whatever other problems he had, at least Satellite was going strong. The venue had built up a crowd of regulars and the name was still spreading. Every week new faces appeared, slick men and fashionably dressed women from as far afield as Croydon and even Essex. The crowd was predominantly black of course but white and Asian ravers were far from unknown. At this rate, Simon reflected, he might have to expand before the end of the year. He saw Cole motioning to him from the main door. Simon took a sip and glanced briefly towards the table to his left where he had been discreetly observing one of the guests. He was sure the woman caught his eyes, but she had looked away so fast...

"That guy there said you told him he could get in free," Cole asked at the gate.

Simon looked at the man in question. He was a tall, light-skinned brother with a stud earring. He seemed to have quite a few girls with him. Simon could vaguely remember talking to him the previous week.

"All these girls with you, man?" he asked.

"Yeah. That's eight of us... I'm the man!"

"You're the man." Simon laughed. "Okay, let him in," he told the large, bald-headed white bouncer he had recently hired. With his recent problems, Simon decided to increase security. Some white friends of his, big timers, had obligingly 'lent' him two heavies.

Simon returned to the bar, everything seemed to be running smoothly tonight. He had planned to hang around a little before making a move with a girl he met the previous week. She hadn't arrived yet, though and Simon didn't really care anymore. He couldn't keep his eyes off the woman sitting near the wall with her companion. The man was of medium height, broad with a thin moustache and a low haircut with left parting, the kind of haircut favoured by Stateside 'top' men. Simon only noticed him because the girl was so beautiful. She wore a two-piece peach designer suit, high-heels and a white silk blouse. Since they arrived over an hour ago, Simon had been sneakily observing her, finding her neat features and rich brown skin very distracting. Two of the women he had just let in had found their way to the bar. They thanked him and engaged in a conversation. After all, he was the boss and that was too good a catch to resist for certain women. They looked nice, Simon had to admit, one in particular whose little black dress hardly concealed her aggresive curves. Yet Simon's mind was on that table to the left, he had caught the woman glancing in his direction only once and he was anxious to find out more about her. He didn't really feel like being upfront and walking up to the table though. From the corner of his eye, he saw the woman get up and walk off towards the ladies room. Simon smiled to himself and politely took leave of his two female companions, then, one hand in his slacks pocket, glass in the other, he worked his way through the crowd towards the end of the bar. He waited and soon enough the woman came back up, easing past the dancers, holding her handbag, progressing Simon's way. He waited until she was level with him then he leaned forward and said over the noise:

"How do you like it?"

The woman hesitated and looked at him. She didn't return his smile.

"Pardon?"

She couldn't hear him, so he moved a little closer to let a couple pass behind him.

"How do you like it?" Simon asked again.

"How do I like what?"

She still looked quite serious.

"The place, all this..." Simon said.

The woman looked at him and asked:

"Why, you're the boss?"

Simon could hear an accent. He nodded.

"Yeah, I am."

The woman shrugged.

"It's okay."

At close quarters she looked even more stunning. Simon realised he was staring.

"You don't dance much," he said.

She shook her head.

"Not tonight, I'm not in the mood."

"Where are you from?" he asked.

She planted those eyes into his.

"Boston," he heard.

"Boston?" he repeated. It was definitely a yankee accent.

"Look, I can't talk right now, okay?" she said.

Then she left him there. Simon was now anxious to find out more. He swallowed the rest of his drink and went back to his vantage point at the other end of the bar. Back at the table, he could see her exchanging words with her companion. She seemed agitated.

Cole came over.

"There's still a queue outside, we're gonna have to turn some out."

"I was just thinking; we need to expand, man. We're too big."

Cole smiled.

"Yeah, let's get a warehouse."

"That's not a bad idea," Simon answered. Then he asked,"You collected from the door?"

Cole nodded. "Yeah, you want that now?"

"No, later."

"I just saw your girl at the back of the queue,"

"What girl?" Simon frowned.

"Your girl from last week, man. You want me to get her in?" Cole asked.

"No man, leave her out there. That ain't my girl."

Simon didn't even want to hear about that. At the table, behind the flow of moving people, he could make out the couple having what looked like an argument. The young American woman said something and turned resolutely away from her companion. Simon saw him get up but a few people hovered by the table, blocking his view. When he saw them again, the man was standing up saying something to the woman. She got up and started to follow him but halfway to the exit door, some ravers got between them. The man back-tracked and Simon saw him take the woman's hand and lead her towards the door. Looking closer he noticed that the man was actually pulling the woman by the wrist and she seemed a little reluctant. Intrigued, Simon climbed down from his stool and followed them. Cole was talking to the barman. Suddenly the girl jerked back her arm, pulling free from the man and began walking back into the club. The man turned around, caught up with her and tried grabbing her arm again. Simon watched the woman, expecting her to pull away but she took a stand and suddenly hit the man in the face with her handbag. Straight after the man slapped her across the face then grabbed the front of her blouse. As she stepped back, trying to resist, the fabric tore. By that time a few people had gathered to watch the fight and Simon was almost there. Cole had followed him and now stood in front of the man as he was literally trying to drag his woman out the door. The man let go of the woman and stepped towards Cole, but then stopped. The big doorman from the front entrance was coming his way. He backed off. Simon had pulled the bruised woman out of the way.

"What's your problem?!" the white bouncer growled at the man.

He didn't have to shout; the voice was deep and gruff enough. The man stiffened, took in the size of the bouncer, noticed the open dinner jacket and caught sight of the hip holster.

"Okay, take it easy. I'm leaving."

Hands held up, he sidestepped towards the door, watching as he went. He didn't even glance in the woman's direction. He pushed quickly out of the door and was gone. Everything returned to normal, Simon led the woman past the dancefloor, through to the back room. He sat her down and got her some mineral water. She wasn't crying, she just looked very angry. Her upper lip was cut. She stemmed the blood flow with a tissue.

"Your boyfriend's kinda ruff, ain't it?" Simon said.

She looked up.

"He's not my boyfriend."

"So what you doing with him?" Simon asked.

The woman sighed.

"It's a complicated story."

"You been here long?" Simon asked her.

The woman winced a little as the tissue touched the cut.

"Three days, but I've been here before."

Simon kept looking at her, making conversation. She was definitely beautiful, even with a cut lip. The woman felt the torn collar of her blouse.

"I need to get to my hotel," she said.

"Where you staying?" Simon asked.

"Notting Hill."

"Okay, I'll drop you off if you want."

She looked at him then got up.

"It's okay, you can call me a taxi."

"I don't mind taking you there, really."

"You sure it's not inconvenient?"

"No, no. I was just gonna leave anyway."

The woman accepted the offer but before leaving she warned: "He might come back, he's dangerous, you know."

"Who? Oh him." Simon laughed. "Don't worry about him. He can't do nothing here."

Simon led the woman out of the room and through the crowd. On the way out he said a few words to Cole. They got outside and walked to the Jaguar parked across the road. The woman kept looking around uneasily.

"Take it easy, you're safe now," Simon said.

He opened the passenger door and let her in. Cole came across the road.

"You're sure you don't want me to come?"

Simon smiled at him.

"Not now, man, this is serious business."

Cole handed him the leather pouch he was carrrying.

"I'll get back to you later," Simon told him, and kicked the engine alive. Beside him, the woman seemed calm. Her lip had started to swell a little.

"This is a really nice car," she said.

Simon sighed satisfyingly.

"Yeah it is." Then he asked, "By the way, what's your name?"

"Oh I'm sorry, I'm Beverley."

"Simon."

He held out his right hand and the woman shook it lightly.

"Thanks for helping me back there."

"Don't mention it, my pleasure," he said, driving out of parking.

A hundred yards away, from his car, Kelly, the man who had been in the club with the American woman, watched the Jaguar's rear lights moving out. He picked up his phone and dialled.

"Yes, don, dem jus' leave. No, him one. Everyt'ing alright... Yeah man, later."

Then he switched on his engine and drove off in the opposite direction. His job was done.

In the Jaguar, things seemed to be going nicely for Simon. He had managed to get the pretty woman to relax and impressed her with a flattering portrait of himself. He wanted to find out much more about her. He asked if she wouldn't mind if he stopped by his house nearby as he didn't want to travel with the money he was carrying. She said that she needed to get cleaned up and changed, but Simon said it would only take a minute. He couldn't help but steal a glance at the woman's long, shapely legs. When he parked by his house, she asked,

189

"You live here?"

"Yeah, it's a quiet area," he said modestly. "Come on, I'll show you around then we'll go to your hotel."

Beverly looked at him for a few seconds then opened the door of the car and got out. She looked around at the impressive houses, the little square opposite. Simon opened the front door and led the way in. He flicked on the lights and walked through into the lounge.

"Have a seat, I won't be long," he said.

"Where's your bathroom?" she asked.

"Down the hall, second left," Simon said from the kitchen. Beverly left her bag on the couch and went to the bathroom. Simon came back in, having put the money in the safe. He caught sight of the abandoned handbag and hesitated a little but still went to peep inside. Nothing much...

Beverly came back, her blouse folded in her arms, her jacket buttoned up. She pushed the garment in her handbag.

"Would you like a drink?" Simon asked.

"No, I don't really drink," she said.

She was looking around the room.

"This is a lovely place."

Simon glowed, feeling confident. It was all working in his favour. He was rather proud of the place.

"Come, I'll show you the study," he said.

He led her into the adjoining room. The woman paused by the two tall, carved African statues, looked at the collection of jade ornaments on one of the shelves, admired the pair of gilded oriental swords crossed on the wall, and had a look at the couple of paintings that adorned the room. It all looked very expensive. Simon pulled the curtains open behind the big black polished desk, revealing the garden. He activated the switch near the window and the garden lights came on. He opened the bay windows. Simon's garden was very pretty, with low, neatly-cut bushes and a pond bordered by flat white stones — across which was a small wooden bridge. A gravel path led through the middle to the tall, wooden gate at the back. Three strategically placed lights projected silhouettes from the Japanese dwarf trees. Beverly looked impressed.

"This is amazing! Who did that?"

Simon had to admit that it wasn't him.

"I've got a Japanese friend. She's very good at landscaping." They went back inside the room. Beverly lifted up the heavy elephant that Simon used as a paperweight on the desk.

"Was this expensive?" she asked.

Simon laughed.

"That's ivory."

She put it down. "You know a lot about art," she remarked.

Outside, D.'s mind wasn't on artistic thoughts. He had watched Simon's car turn the corner. It was his time now. He didn't want to leave Bess in there too long, she had done good. He waited a few minutes more then told Slinga:

"Alright; I gwan park de car in front of de back alley. You keep watch on de front, when Lancey come, yuh call in."

"What if Lancey go t'rough de back?"

D. looked at Slinga.

"I feel seh him gwan go t'rough de lickle room downstairs," he said.

He made sure Slinga knew his number and gave him Charlie's mobile which he had borrowed earlier on. Slinga climbed out and went to set watch behind some cars opposite the house. Then D. drove to the alley and backed out just near the entrance. That way he could get away fast. Then he started up the narrow alley, counting the gates to get to the right house. The fence was tall — made of wood plants, tightly battened together. One smaller metal door was the garage. The garden gate had a small door, locked from the inside. D. adjusted the gun in his belt and breathed in deeply. The alley was silent. There were only a few lights from the adjoining houses but it was quite dark. In his mind D. hoped one last time that Bess had managed to get the back door open, otherwise it was going to be noisy. He jumped up and scaled the fence easily, then balanced himself before jumping down. Thirty yards away, from where he was crouching, he could see a man, back to the garden, sitting in a chair and Bess perched on the corner of the desk beside him. He had to be swift. Treading lightly on the short lawn, eyes set on the room and his gun in his right hand, D. tiptoed towards the bay window, keeping to the side at first. Then he stepped on the gravel path, trying not to make any noise. He was just a yard or so away from the room when the small pebbles creaked under his feet. He saw Simon turn halfway towards him and knew he had seen his shadow. Immediately Simon's hand flew to the top drawer of his desk, but Bess had seen D. before he had. She was ready. All in one move, she grabbed the ivory elephant from the desk and smashed it on Simon's wrist as he tried to pull something from the drawer. He cried out in pain. The next thing he knew, the barrel of D.'s automatic was up against his temple. Simon froze. With his left hand, D. pulled out a large printed fabric kerchief from his back pocket. He handed it to Bess.

"Use dis wipe up any prints."

D. was working fast. He undid Simon's tie and proceeded to

tie up the man's hand behind his back with it. Simon was sweating profusely. He couldn't even look straight at D., now standing at the desk, a scowl on his face.

"Long time me wan' see yuh," D. said simply. Then he turned to Bess and asked:

"Yuh alright?"

"Yeah man, me cool."

She seemed composed enough. Next, D. took out his phone and dialled. He gave Simon's address, listened then hung up. If Joseph had done his work well, everything was now programmed. The bait was in place. Simon's throat was dry, his head empty. Bess told D.:

"Him bring in some money."

D. looked down at Simon and nudged him in the head with the barrel of the gun.

"Hey bwoy, whe' de safe deh?"

Simon looked up and swallowed. At that particular moment, money was the last thing on his mind.

"In the kitchen," he mumbled.

D. grabbed him by the collar and pulled.

"Which part?" he asked coldly, his eyes inches from Simon's.

Simon swallowed harder and hissed.

"Under the sink."

D. pushed him back down onto the chair and went to check out the information. He came back.

"What's the combination?" he asked.

Simon told him right away. D. tried it and it worked. He returned with a wicked grin and tossed several thick wads of money onto the desk. In his hand was a squarish plastic wrapper.

"Yuh 'ave everyt'ing, bwoy!" he smirked at Simon as he set down the parcel in front of him.

Then he sat on the corner of the desk and put down his gun beside the elephant. Bess was standing by his side.

Yuh bettah leave now," D. told her, "I will tek care of everyt'ing."

"Me haffe stay wid yuh," she said resolutely.

D. gave her a deep look but didn't insist. He pulled his knife from his pocket, Simon gasped. He was literally shaking with fear now, even too terrified to plead.

"So yuh kill people, but yuh 'fraid to die," D. said.

Simon spoke for the first time, in a raspish voice.

"It wasn't me."

D. yanked Simon by the back of the neck and held the blade under his throat.

"Who pulled the trigger on Sticks?"

Simon jerked his head back as he felt the sharp blade against his skin, but the tall chair trapped it.

"Talk, man." D.'s dark eyes were focused deep into Simon's, who was trying everything to avert them.

"I... I... Some people did it."

"Who?" D. asked, the blade digging a little further into Simon's throat.

"My friend."

D.'s face was a mask, no movement, no expression.

"Yuh is a pussy," he spat, "yuh cyan look ina man eye an' kill him."

A little flick of his wrist brought a cry from Simon. Bess thought D. was about to cut his throat right there and then. D. actually felt that way but he remembered the plan. He had to spare him for now.

D. picked up the bag of white powder from the desk and tossed it in the palm of his hand.

"Yuh ah rich bwoy; nice house, nice car, money... but yuh

dead now. Yuh cyan buy notin' again."

Simon wanted to say something, wanted to bargain. But deep inside he knew the man in front of him couldn't be bought. He had heard about him but always thought that D. would never get to him. He knew now he had been wrong in thinking that once his soldiers were out of the way, D. would be weak. He watched as D. made a little cut in the plastic bag and tipped some powder on the edge of his blade. The stereo Simon had switched on earlier was still dispensing soft soul music. D. brought the blade up right in front of his face, looking sideways at the little white mound on the tip. But it wasn't for him. He pushed the blade under Simon's nose.

"Sniff it," he ordered.

Simon's eyes opened wide. D. pushed the blade right under the man's left nostril and pressed it in.

"Sniff!" he ordered again. So Simon did. Bess was still standing motionless, watching. D. picked up some more coke, ordered again.

"Sniff!"

For the next few minutes he repeatedly dipped the tip of the blade in the bag of cocaine forcing Simon to snort every time. D. could see uncontrolable terror in Simon's eyes. He gave him more powder, pushing it in with his blade when the man hesitated. Then Simon pleaded.

"Please..."

That got D. upset. He grabbed Simon by his ponytail and yanked hard.

"I don't wan' hear no beggin', seen? Try to die like a man." Then he smirked. "I comin' like dentist. I give yuh somet'ing fe your nerves."

Simon was cracking up. He was sniffing, coughing and sweating all at the same time. Unperturbed, D. lifted up his blade again. This time he insisted:

"Open your mouth."

Simon was trembling And breathing heavily. He mumbled something but the edge of D.'s blade was right against his lips, almost cutting.

"Open man, or I cut it open."

The state he was in, Simon had no doubt D. would do it. His stomach was tight, fear gripping it like a claw. He didn't want to shake, he didn't want to be afraid but his whole body was twitching in terror. Prodded on by the sharp tip of D.'s blade, he opened his mouth. D. poured the powder down into his throat. Pricking him on the chin, he ordered:

"Eat it, man. Fast!"

Simon swallowed and coughed, tears rolling down now. He tried to plead again but D. frowned and forced him to swallow a second bladeful. By the third mouthful, Simon was coughing seriously, spluttering and breathing heavily. But D. was unmoved. Simon's chest heaved up and down, cocaine mixed with saliva and phlegm running down the corner of his mouth, dripping onto his shirt. D. picked up the plastic bag and held it over Simon's head, shaking it. The powder trickled over the man's head and face. D. shook his head, put the bag down.

"Me t'ink seh yuh ah bad bwoy, but yuh is jus' a lickle informer, a pussyhole."

He made as if to stab Simon in the eye. The man cried out:
"No!!"

Disgusted, D. left Simon there and went downstairs to check out the rest of the house. He found one bedroom, one bathroom and toilet, plus a cupboard. The small bedroom window was level with the street, looking out towards the park. D. went back upstairs. Simon was in a bad way, his eyes were closed. He kept coughing and his mouth was dribbling.

D. pricked him on the cheek with his knife and opened his eyes. They looked glazed.

"Drug abuse," D. said to Bess seriously...

It had all looked straightforward on the map but Lancey had somehow missed the turn. He drove on towards the petrol station a little further down to ask his way. According to Joseph, he would be just in time to catch the deal as it was going down, and D...

The first call the previous day had shaken Lancey out of the brooding mood he'd been in for the past week. He was smarting from the way he had been insulted and because none of his moves to get D. had worked. Yet Joseph's call had not really surprised him; someone always informed in this game. Once he had worked out Joseph's motives, it all made a lot of sense for him to want to give up D. After all, he would 'inherit' his rival's territory, it was a cunning move. Lancey got out of the car and went to get directions...

Inside the house, Simon was in a bad way, his head flopping from left to right, his eyes half-open. D. had forced him to ingest more cocaine. He had even retched on his shirt. Bess still hadn't moved, but stood by the desk, watching dispassionately as Simon suffered. The ring of D.'s mobile interrupted him. He picked it up and listened.

"Yeah... a'right. Go to the car."

He looked at Bess and hung up.

"Hide behind de desk, don't move."

Bess obeyed and crouched down beside Simon's chair. D. had figured right; Lancey was entering from the basement room. He folded back the knife and picked up his gun from the desk.

On his way to the next room he turned the lights down low. Then he went to hide against the wall unit near the top of the stairs. The place was silent but for the music playing low. After a few minutes, D. heard the creaking of wood. He held his breath and waited. He couldn't afford any mistake, he had to be fast. Soon the back of Lancey's head appeared on the stairwell. Slowly the man climbed up the stairs watching, listening. D. could see Lancey scanning the space around him. D. saw him stop as he noticed the figure sitting at the desk in the adjoining room. That was what D. was waiting for. Swiftly he moved from behind the unit and in one quick step was behind Lancey, pushing his gun in the back of the man's neck.

"Don't try."

Lancey froze, D. wrenched the revolver from his grasp and pushed him forward with the barrel of his own weapon. Lancey stepped into the next room facing Simon. He was trying to work it all out but Simon was in no state to answer any questions. D. came from behind, Lancey still covered with his gun, and walked back towards the desk. He motioned Bess to come out. Lancey glared at her. D. sat on the edge of the desk and sized up his enemy.

"I hear seh yuh ah look fe me; see me yah!"

Lancey shrugged.

"D. man, ah small problem dat. Mek we reason nuh?"

He tried to gain some ground after his initial surprise.

"Reason? After yuh bust ina my woman yard wid gun?"

D. was glaring at the policeman, filled with bad intentions. Standing in the middle of the room dressed in another one of his blue suits, Lancey didn't answer. He looked around, visibly uncomfortable. Eventually his eyes returned to D.

"You set me up," he said.

D. smirked.

"Glad yuh could come to de party. See money yah, see coke..." He motioned towards the desk with his gun.

Lancey's brain was working fast. He knew D. wouldn't hesitate.

"Look D., de whole ah we ah businessman. I know seh yuh vex wid me, but we can 'gotiate somet'ing, nuh true?"

Typical Lancey, still trying to make a deal. D. pointed at him with the gun.

"Yuh is not a businessman, yuh is a police bwoy, an' a scavenger. Dat is all yuh is." He paused. "It's over fe yuh, Lancey. Yuh kill 'nuff people, but tonight is your turn."

Lancey stared at D., visibly shaken but trying to keep cool. He looked at Simon again, still shocked at the way he had been fooled. Suddenly the front door bell rang. D. frowned and looked at Bess. Before he could react the girl was moving forward to go and check the door. D. realised immediately the danger but he was too late to prevent it from happening. Lancey was fast. Bess had only taken two steps forward before Lancey dived on her. Quickly, he grabbed her by the throat and, lifting her from the waist with one arm stepped backwards rapidly. D. took aim but Lancey held Bess tight in front of him, his large hand choking her by the throat. He grabbed one of the curved decorative knives from the wall with his free hand. D.'s mind emptied as he stood helplessly watching Lancey, a few yards away, holding the large blade against Bess' slender neck.

"Easy D., easy. T'row down de gun, or she dead."

D.'s gun was still trained on Lancey but he couldn't risk a shot. Bess was still, her head tilted upwards by the pressure from the knife. The bell rang again.

"T'row me de gun, man. Now!" Lancey ordered. Bess stiffened as the blade cut into her skin, but she didn't make a sound. D. sighed, his eyes focused hard on Lancey's. He lowered his gun, hesitated then threw it down, but not towards Lancey. He sent the weapon sliding towards the wall to his right, too far for Lancey to reach. The police man laughed, a hollow evil laugh.

"Yuh nuh wan' lend me your gun. Alright, now tek out my gun, slowly. T'row it my way," Lancey said, adding, "don't get brave or your girl lose her t'roat."

Slowly D. eased up Lancey's revolver from his waist and tossed it down on the carpet in front of the man. Rapidly, Lancey grabbed it and dropped the knife. He let go of Bess. She quickly stepped towards D. Oblivious to all this, Simon was still semi-conscious sitting at the desk. Lancey had the whole room covered. He smiled.

"Yuh expect more guests?" he asked D. His sense of humour had returned. There was the sound of the street door closing, then a voice called:

"Simon!"

At the same time, Cole walked into the living room. Because the light was turned low he couldn't quite make out what was going on in the study and was already committed before he realised something was wrong. Simon was at the desk but seemed to be sleeping, then Cole noticed the couple standing by the desk and when he turned to his right, his eyes fixed on Lancey's gun and sarcastic grin. Cole's face dropped.

"Yuh late, de party start a'ready."

Lancey pushed Cole in towards the wall. He ended up a few feet away from D. to his right. He looked shocked and quickly realised that something serious was going down. Somehow he couldn't keep his eyes off Simon's white-blotched face.

"You killed him!" he said.

Lancey laughed.

200

"Him not dead yet." Then he said, "I did warn yuh to keep yuh mout' shut, remember?"

Cole was standing, his arm by his side.

"I didn't say nothing," he insisted.

"Your friend is a informer, I know dat. But him shouldn't inform against me."

D. was staring at Cole too. Although it was Simon he had really wanted, he knew now that this man was the one who actually shot Sticks. The set-up had worked and all his enemies were together in the room, only he wasn't the one holding the gun. Lancey kissed his teeth. He had caught sight of the money on the table and asked:

"So, who buyin' de drugs?"

He looked at D., D. said nothing. He knew one way or another, some people were not going to leave the room alive and although things seemed tipped against him, as always there had to be a way out...

Lancey gave Cole a suspicious look, remembering something.

"Lif' up yuh shirt."

Cole didn't move.

"Lif' up yuh shirt!" Lancey's tone was urgent, the revolver in his hand pointing.

Ashen-faced, Cole hitched up his shirt, revealing the heavy-looking butt in his waist. Lancey shook his head and made a throat noise.

"I did give yuh a chance..."

His eyes wandered to Simon at his desk, to Bess, to D. standing with his back to the garden and with death in his eyes, then back to Cole.

"Drug deal gone wrong..."

Cole didn't understand right away what the policeman meant by that. He watched stupefied, as Lancey's eyes turned

201

towards Simon. Cole's mouth opened to utter a cry but the shot rang out before he had even formed the words.

"No!" he shouted, as Lancey's bullet bore a neat hole into his friend's forehead. Simon's head dropped to one side, permanently. D didn't move, Bess stiffened but kept still. The gun in Lancey's hand circled past them without stopping then thundered as the second shot hit Cole in the face. Blood squirted on the wall behind as he dropped to the floor, dead.

As soon as Lancey shot Simon, D. knew what was coming. His mind ticked on overdrive as the black barrel pointed towards him ready to spit out its death. He had no chance of making it to his gun laying on the floor just out of reach. Behind him were the open doors to the garden... Though he had a chance of making it out, D. couldn't sacrifice Bess. The .38 was on him now, Lancey's eyes cold as the steel inside it. The barrel inched towards Bess as Lancey said:

"Dem don't matter to me, is you I come for..."

D. didn't need to see the trigger squeezed to know the shot was coming. He stopped thinking, turned sharply to his left and threw himself at Bess, wrestling her to the ground behind the desk. As she fell against Simon's chair and to the floor, D. heard the 'bang' of the gun and almost at the same time, a burning bolt hit him in the side. One more shot rang out, a second bolt drilled into his back under the right shoulder, as he crashed down. He heard Bess yelling.

"D...! D...!!"

She felt his limp body fall on top of her, then slide sideways, ending up spreadeagled on his back. Bess didn't lose control, her mind already numbed by the ninety seconds of slaughter she had just lived through. D. had just saved her, but for how long? Lancey would finish the job any moment now... As she crouched behind the desk, Bess noticed a shiny object which

202

had fallen out of the desk drawer D. had dragged down with his fall. Simon's gun, the one she had prevented him from reaching for earlier on! The small, silver revolver stood out against the dark carpet, near the open garden door. Only a few seconds had passed since Lancey's last shot rang out. From under the desk, Bess saw Lancey's feet coming her way. She didn't consciously decide to move but somehow found herself reaching for the gun, out of fear. Still on her knees, she wrapped her right hand around it, feeling the trigger. She lifted her left hand to support the other. Lancey was standing over the desk now. He stopped as he saw the slender, frightened woman with the small revolver looking up at him. His own weapon was trained on her. He glanced briefly at D., very still, eyes closed.

"Gimme de gun!" Lancey barked.

He could see she was shaky. Bess fixed her eyes into his, she lowered her hands slightly.

"Hey gal, gimme de bloodclaat gun, now!" he thundered.

Right at that moment a noise made him turn towards the garden gate. Slinga's face appeared over the top as he pulled himself up. Lancey was already taking aim, unlikely to miss at such a short distance. Atop the gate, Slinga dived forward to avoid the shot.

Bess saved his life. She didn't pause to consider what had distracted Lancey. Driven by her own emotional reaction to the massacre she had just witnessed, she raised the gun again and squeezed once, twice, three times...

The first shot hit Lancey in the side of the neck, he stepped back and turned towards the woman with a shocked look on his face. The two other bullets hit him square in the chest and he fell backwards. He struggled to get back up, still clinging to his gun. Then his hand went to his neck from where blood gushed freely all over his blue jacket.

Slinga stepped in, guns at the ready, just in time to witness Lancey's last convulsion. Her eyes closed, her jaws tight, Bess still held the gun tight. D. moaned. She dropped the weapon and crawled to him. Slinga looked around the room.

"Everybody dead," he said. Then tucking his gun in his waist, he helped Bess lift D. to his feet.

The pain in his chest was terrible, but D. struggled to balance upright. It felt like a cramp had stiffened his entire body. He looked down at Lancey; he knew he was dead by the way his eyes stared upwards.

"My gun..." D. muttered.

Slinga looked and found D.'s gun and tucked it away. D. pointed to the small revolver on the carpet, Slinga picked it up.

"Untie him." D. motioned

Slinga turned to Simon and untied his hands from behind his back.

"Give him de gun." D.'s voice was weak, he coughed.

"Come on, D.; let's go!" Bess said urgently, propping him up, one arm around his waist. They shuffled out to the garden while Slinga wrapped Simon's dead fingers around the gun.

"Tek my bag, and the 'kerchief...!" Bess called out to Slinga as she walked D. to the garden gate.

Slinga caught up with them and unbolted the door. They had to leave fast, the shots would have woken up the neighbours.

With D. supported on either side, they walked up the alley towards the car. D. felt his strength leaving him, his throat was dry and his head hot. Sweat had covered his whole body. Slinga opened the back door of the BMW and helped D. in while Bess, from the other side, pulled him into the vehicle. Then Slinga took the wheel and started the engine. The car lurched forward as he slipped it into gear, then stopped, then jumped again. D. winced.

"Wha'ppen; yuh cyan drive?" Bess asked him sharply.

Slinga tried again and this time got the car moving.

"I nevah drive stick before."

He got to the main road and soon had the hang of it. At the back, Bess cradled D.'s head in her lap. He was still, his eyes open, his breath shallow but still fighting the pain.

"You hang on, D... Don't give up, yuh hear me? Don't give up."

It was only then that she felt the warm tears streaming down her face.

The passengers emerging from behind the automatic doors were dressed appropriately. This year, summer in England was much like the sunny climes they had left behind in Jamaica. Some were waving excitedly to awaiting relatives and friends, others simply strolled along at the unhurried pace they had gotten used to during their holiday. Eventually, they came through; Donna pushing a loaded trolley, Avril by her side, Cindy behind under a large straw hat and carrying a backpack and a basket. They got to the end of the line. Marcus was already running up to them, he smiled at Avril. Charlie picked up the little girl and kissed her.

"You're getting fat!" he teased as he put her down.

He kissed Cindy, greeted Donna and took the trolley from her.

"Where is D.?" she asked.

"He couldn't make it," Charlie answered without looking at her.

Donna frowned, put one hand over Charlie's arm, stopping him.

"Charlie, tell me what happen?" she demanded. "Somet'ing happen to D...?!"

A young man passed them, he recognised Charlie and smiled enigmatically but kept on walking. Pulling his suitcase behind him, he called out.

"Yes, Star! Cyan stop, seen?! Later!" he said with a knowing wink and marched on.

Charlie turned to Donna.

"Take it easy, Donna. Let's get out of here first."

He started back towards the exit, Donna and the children following.

The End.

Victor Headley

Yardie   £3.99

At Heathrow Airport's busy Immigration desk, a newly-arrived Jamaican strolls through with a kilo of top-grade cocaine strapped to his body. And keeps on walking . . .

By the time the syndicate get to hear about the missing consignment, D is in business – for himself – as the Front Line's newest don.

But D's treachery will never be forgotten – or forgiven. The message filters down from the Yardie crime lords to their soldiers on the streets:

Find D. Find the merchandise. And make him pay for his sins . . .

'A book which everyone should read, and soon'

The Voice

'Who said you need a review in the quality Sundays to have a hit?'

City Limits

'The black Godfather . . . quite simply, Headley knows what time it is'

The Journal

'It's the ruffest, the tuffest and the boo-yacka of all modern gangster novels'

Caribbean Times

Victor Headley

Excess   **£4.99**

EXCESS – the devastating sequel to *Yardie*. Where the road to hell is paved with *bad* intentions . . .

D had hit the streets like a one-man war zone. Now he's doing time. But putting him away hasn't stopped the killing. Among the Yardie crime lords the real battle for power is only just beginning . . .

The law think they've closed down Hackney for business. But the shaky truce can't last . . . not while there's still operators prepared to take chances with other people's crack . . .

Meanwhile D's legacy lives on. One woman gives births to his daughter, another to his son. In the middle of the mayhem, the battle of the sexes was one war the Don hadn't figured on fighting . . .

'A unique take on London's seamy, violent underbelly . . . scorching'

Time Out

'Fast-moving as ever and essential reading'

ID

'Victor Headley is a breath of fresh air on the stale literary scene'

The Face

'*Excess* will make *Yardie* look like Noddy's day out'
Touch Magazine

Walter Mosley

Black Betty   £4.99

'Saul Lynx had a smile that was just about as sincere as the kind of grin the undertaker puts on a corpse. "Have you ever heard of a woman named Elizabeth Eady?" he asked'

Five years have passed since the white butterfly affair: there's a Kennedy in the White House and Martin Luther King is in the news. It might look like a new dawn but for Easy Rawlins times are only getting tougher – his real-estate empire is deep in the hole.

And then, sure enough, trouble comes knocking again at Easy's door when he is asked to find a missing woman, the stunningly beautiful Elizabeth Eady, aka 'Black Betty'.

'Betty was a great shark of a woman. Men died in her wake'

'Mosley is already outstripping the genre. Stay with him while you can'

Literary Review

Shortlisted for the 1994 Golden Dagger Award

All Pan Books are available at your local bookshop or newsagent, or can be ordered direct from the publisher. Indicate the number of copies required and fill in the form below.

Send to: Macmillan General Books C.S.
                Book Service By Post
                PO Box 29, Douglas I-O-M
                IM99 1BQ

or phone: 01624 675137, quoting title, author and credit card number.

or fax: 01624 670923, quoting title, author, and credit card number.

Please enclose a remittance* to the value of the cover price plus 75 pence per book for post and packing. Overseas customers please allow £1.00 per copy for post and packing.

*Payment may be made in sterling by UK personal cheque, Eurocheque, postal order, sterling draft or international money order, made payable to Book Service By Post.

Alternatively by Access/Visa/MasterCard

Card No. ☐☐☐☐☐☐☐☐☐☐☐☐☐☐☐☐☐☐☐☐☐

Expiry Date ☐☐☐☐☐☐☐☐☐☐☐☐☐☐☐☐☐☐☐☐☐

Signature _____

Applicable only in the UK and BFPO addresses.

While every effort is made to keep prices low, it is sometimes necessary to increase prices at short notice. Pan Books reserve the right to show on covers and charge new retail prices which may differ from those advertised in the text or elsewhere.

NAME AND ADDRESS IN BLOCK CAPITAL LETTERS PLEASE

Name _____

Address _____

_____

_____

_____

3/95

Please allow 28 days for delivery.
Please tick box if you do not wish to receive any additional information. ☐